Also by Natasha D. Frazier

<u>Devotionals</u>

<u>The Life Your Spirit Craves</u>

<u>Not Without You</u>

<u>Not Without You Prayer Journal</u>

<u>The Life Your Spirit Craves for Mommies</u>

<u>Pursuit</u>

<u>Fiction</u>

<u>Love, Lies & Consequences</u>

<u>Through Thick & Thin: Love, Lies & Consequences Book 2</u>

<u>Shattered Vows: Love, Lies & Consequences Book 3</u>

<u>Out of the Shadows: Love, Lies & Consequences Book 4</u>

<u>Kairos: The Perfect Time for Love</u>

<u>Fate (The Perfect Time for Love series)</u>

<u>With Every Breath (McCall Family Series Book 1)</u>

<u>With Every Step (McCall Family Series Book 2)</u>

<u>Non-Fiction</u>

<u>How Long Are You Going to Wait?</u>

Copyright © 2022 by Natasha D. Frazier

Published by Encouraging Works

Printed by Ingram Spark

ISBN: 978-0-9994496-7-7

Scripture quotations are taken from the *New King James Version*. Copyright © 1982, 1992 by Thomas Nelson, Inc. Used by permission. All rights reserved.

This is a work of fiction. Names, characters, businesses, places, events, and incidents are either the products of the author's imagination or used in a fictitious manner. Any resemblance to actual persons, living or dead, or actual events is purely coincidental.

Editor: Chandra Sparks Splond

For autographed copies, please visit:

www.natashafrazier.com

Acknowledgements

The excitement I get from releasing a new title never gets old.

My biggest thank you is to Jesus, who orders my steps, forgives my sins, and blesses me with the time and ability to do the thing I love – write. As time goes on, I'm even more thankful for the time and opportunity to share my stories with you.

To my mom, who never misses an opportunity to tell the world that she's proud of me, thank you for your support.

My husband, Eddie, and my children Eden, Ethan, and Emilyn – thank you for sharing me with my characters. I know this isn't always easy to do, so I am grateful for your sacrifice.

Chandra – Thank you for your editing expertise. You are, indeed, the best.

My dearest reader – Thank you for reading, reviewing, and sharing my books with others. I am thankful for you and your support. I hope you enjoy (what I think is) the final installment of the McCall family. I've enjoyed spending time with them, and I hope you have as well. Your support of this series has been mind-blowing—thank you!

Natasha

With Every Moment

McCall Family Series Book 3

With Every Moment

ONE

Will you marry me?

The Christmas holiday season hadn't been the same in five years for Danielle Adams–all because everything about it reminded her of her ex, Michael Stewart. He adored everything about the season. Movies. Music. The miracle of Jesus' birth. Time with family. Light shows. Peppermint chocolate chip cookies. The list could go on forever. To top it off, he proposed during the Christmas season.

And they were engaged for about two weeks, then she gave the ring back.

Each year around this time, she regretted that decision more and more. But this year should be different.

Her nine-month relationship with Brandon Banks had been nothing short of amazing, yet thoughts of Mike still ran rampant in her mind. Could it be because she would see him later this afternoon?

She hadn't been able to stop thinking about how he'd react to seeing her after five years since Nina invited her to the McCall Resorts ribbon-cutting ceremony.

Forget Mike's response. How would she react?

"Babe, did you hear me?" Brandon reached across the breakfast table and took both of her hands into his.

Danielle jerked, not quite sure how much of the conversation she'd missed. "I'm sorry for being so distracted. I'm all ears now. Say it again."

He massaged the back of her hands. "You sure you're okay? Anything we need to talk about?"

"No. I'm all good. What's on your mind?" Danielle took a deep breath and relaxed under his touch.

Brandon flashed that smile she'd fallen for, and her heart flip-flopped. Whatever he was about to say had to be a big deal.

She held her breath.

"I'd like to introduce you to my parents this Christmas. I know we've talked about the next step, and I think we're ready. We're good together, and you're a special part of my life."

Can't this wait until after Christmas?

She didn't want to jinx their relationship. Would she and Brandon suffer the same fate as her and Mike if they made this a Christmas thing? Would creating this memory with Brandon erase the Christmas memories she had with Mike?

She wasn't ready.

"Can we talk about it more this evening?"

His shoulders slumped, but he hid his disappointment with a smile.

"We can do that. Over dinner. I'll cook tonight."

"Sounds good."

Danielle made it through the rest of brunch without talk of their future together before she made a beeline out of Toasted Yolk to drive across town for the grand opening.

Had this been any other time of the year, last month, or even next month, she may have agreed to meet his parents when he asked, but right now, all she could think about was Mike. And it wouldn't be right for her to spend this time with him when Mike dominated her thoughts.

Maybe after seeing Mike today, she could flush him out of her system and move on.

∞

I wish you were here to see this.

The cool December breeze kissed Mike Stewart's face as he lifted his eyes toward heaven. Slaughter Construction, Inc. had completed its largest construction contract since inception for McCall Resorts an hour outside of Houston, Texas. The forty-two-hundred acre luxury resort would bring in tourists from all over the country and many jobs for the locals. His late best friend and SCI's founder, Kendrick Slaughter, would have loved to see SCI take on a project of this size.

Mike strolled toward the five-story office building, chest inflated, with a smile as shiny as the newly installed glass. He skirted around the red oversized grand opening ribbon and went inside to meet his long-time friend and boss, Kennedy Slaughter, along with the McCall Resorts team.

4

With Every Moment

Goosebumps popped up on his arms when he entered. Christmas music played throughout the building. Wreaths, garland, and red velvety bows hung along the walls. This was his favorite time of the year, and knowing that they'd accomplished something as huge as this project made it even better.

"Mike, you look like a million bucks." Kennedy rushed to his side and threw her arms around his neck. "We did it. This resort is amazing."

Mike glanced around the modern open space. Glass offices and conference rooms. Recessed lighting. A spiral staircase. A small lounge area outside of the reception area. "It really is a sight to see."

"Ken would be so proud. I just wish he could see this." Kennedy's voice was low and reminiscent, but he heard her and understood.

If no one else got it, he did. Kendrick's dream was to become the most successful privately owned construction company in Texas. A dream he shared with his twin sister, Kennedy, and Mike at every opportunity.

Mike rubbed his hand along her back, took a deep breath, and released it. "Well, I know one thing. He'd be proud of you. We all are."

"He's right. SCI is lucky to have you." His mom, Mabel Stewart, stepped in between them and wrapped her arms around both of their waists.

Kennedy's eyelids fluttered, and she offered one of those smiles where he could tell she was fighting back tears.

"Thanks."

She led them over to the McCall team and greeted them with handshakes. "The news outlets are pulling up now to prepare for the ribbon cutting. Who else are you all expecting?"

Andrew McCall's wife, Nina McCall, piped in, bouncing their son, Andrew Jr., in her arms. "My assistant, Danielle, should arrive soon. I can't wait for her to see this place. We're also waiting for Uncle Thad. I don't think he's bringing anyone since he and Liz are no longer together."

Nina may have uttered something else along with a few others from the McCall clan, but when he heard Danielle's name, his heart stopped. Nina may as well have thrust her fist to his chest and knocked the air out of him. He hadn't laid eyes on *his* Danielle in five years. To know within minutes that he'd see her again made everything inside of him clench.

He wasn't ready.

Mike had to be certain. "Excuse me, Nina. You mean Danielle Adams, right?"

"Yes."

Nina covered her mouth with her free hand and widened her eyes in recognition. "Oh, my gosh. I knew something about you was familiar when we met earlier this year. You and Danielle were involved at one time, right?"

Involved may have been putting it lightly. He'd proposed before their relationship ended.

He cleared his throat. "Right."

"I need to call and let her know you'll be here. When I invited her, I wasn't thinking."

Mike reached out and squeezed Nina's arm. "It's okay. It'll be nice to see her and catch up after all this time."

Nina squinted for a moment, but seemed satisfied with his response.

7

"Alright."

She whispered something in Kennedy's ear before rejoining her family.

Kennedy folded her arms across her chest. Her gaze roamed from his head to his feet. His mother stood in a similar stance.

"Okay, so how do you really feel about seeing Danielle again?"

Mike stuffed his hands into his pockets. "Honestly, I don't know. There were never any hard feelings when things ended. I understood she was going through a rough time."

Mabel nodded toward the door. "Well, here's your chance to find out."

Mike shifted to face the entrance, and the Christmas song playing through the room and the team's chatter ceased. She smiled, which he liked to believe was at him, and waved. He had to restrain every muscle in his body to keep from running to Danielle and wrapping his arms around her. Instead, he strolled a few feet in her direction and extended his hand.

"So good to see you, Danielle." She accepted his handshake. His palm remembered the familiar warmth that slid up his arm. His chest strained from his heart's gallop. He couldn't let go. "Still beautiful. How've you been?"

"Michael Thaddeus Stewart."

"Stop, it. You know I prefer Mike."

Danielle smirked. "I remember everything about you. I was hoping we'd run into each other today. When Nina invited me and mentioned SCI did the construction, you were the first thing that came to mind."

Mike bit his bottom lip while his eyes roamed her slender five-foot, two-inch frame. Though five years had passed, everything about her remained the same.

The way her eyes captivated him.

The way his heart responded to her presence, like it was filled with helium.

The way being near her made everything alright in his world.

Except it wasn't. Because she wasn't part of it.

He released her and tucked his hand away in his pocket.

No matter what she said, they weren't an item. And after today, he likely wouldn't see her for another five years.

"It's nice to see you. I'll let you get to Nina now. Enjoy the ceremony."

"Thanks." Danielle spun on her heel, but turned to look over her shoulder and asked, "Would you like to catch up over coffee when this is over?"

Though tempted to decline and leave the past where it belonged, he agreed. Her eyes convinced him. "Yeah, I would. I'll come find you."

Danielle nodded and walked away to join Nina and her family. Mike's head ached from the holes Kennedy's and Mabel's eyes burned into his skull.

Mabel was the first to speak. "Michael Thaddeus Stewart, I thought you were giving up coffee."

But I still love Dani.

"I'll be okay, Mom. No worries."

He reached out to reassure her, but her mouth continued to hang open in shock.

"Mom, I really am fine."

∞

With Every Moment

Mike avoided the Danielle conversation with his mom because her eyes were glued to someone behind him. He turned to see who had her attention. The man, who he assumed to be with the McCall family, stopped in his tracks and locked eyes with Mabel. Mike had never met him, but sensed something familiar about him. The man now looked from Mike to Mabel with raised eyebrows.

"Mom, is everything okay?"

"Mabel Stewart?"

"Thaddeus Williams?"

The man rushed toward her and swooped her up into his arms and held her for much longer than Mike liked, garnering the attention of everyone else in the building. When he released her, he looked from her to Mike, and Mabel dipped her chin and averted her eyes.

"It's Thaddeus McCall now." He spoke slowly, still looking from her to Mike. "I changed it to my adopted family's name when I graduated from medical school."

Mike now looked at the two of them, and they couldn't seem to tear their eyes away from each other.

"How do you know him?"

"Oh, I'm sorry, Mike. This is Thaddeus McCall, also known as Thad. Thad, this is my son, Mike."

"Nice to meet you, Mike." Thaddeus shook his hand and looked him straight in the eyes—eyes that seemed familiar, like they shared a connection. But that was strange, considering he'd never met the man.

Thaddeus tore his eyes away from Mike and focused on Mabel. "I haven't seen you in what…thirty-eight years?"

"Yes. It's been a long time. My mom thought it was best if I moved here to stay with my grandmother."

He took both of her hands in his. "But you left without so much as a phone call or letter. You disappeared."

"I know. I had to. It was for the best. You were going to medical school and…" Her words trailed off.

Mike looked from one to the other. His mind raced, putting pieces together of a puzzle he didn't know existed.

"Wait a minute," Mike said.

Mabel's gaze remained zoned in on Thaddeus, but she reached for Mike's hand. "Hold on, son. Can the three of us step away to talk?"

Thaddeus nodded his agreement, but Mike stood, paralyzed, his body numb, his lips unable to part. He somehow knew what she would say, but didn't know if he could stay there to listen.

Had his whole life been a lie?

Mabel tugged Mike into the nearest office with Thaddeus following close behind and shut the door. Tears filled her eyes. She fidgeted with her fingers—something he'd never witnessed her doing. Even with his father, she'd always been strong, much different from the nervous, faltering woman before him.

Mike plopped down into a cushioned leather seat. "I need to hear you say it. Tell me my whole life has been a lie."

Tears poured from her eyes like salt from a canister. "I–I–I'm sorry."

Thaddeus must have figured out the truth because he'd turned away from her and leaned against the window frame. Nothing to see but green pastures.

"Thirty-eight years, and you couldn't pick up the phone? Technology is advanced enough now that there is no excuse. I deserved more." He spun on his heel and thrust his finger toward Mike. "He deserved more."

"I thought I was doing what was best for all of us."

"By not telling me I have a son?"

Thaddeus' thundering voice drew attention from the rest of the family. Rose McCall, his sister-in-law, and matriarch of the McCall family, tapped on the door. "Is everything alright?"

Thaddeus called to her, not attempting to mask his hurt and anger. "Give us a minute, Rose."

Mabel sniffed, and her voice cracked. "I know there's no excuse that will satisfy either of you. Please forgive me."

Mike leaped from his seat and stormed out of the room. He didn't stop to say goodbye to anyone before he raced out of the building. Now didn't seem like the proper time to celebrate this career milestone when his world had just been turned upside down.

He trotted past the news reporters and their vehicles to his SUV. He climbed inside, turned the ignition, and looked toward heaven.

With Every Moment

As a matter of fact, Ken, I'm glad you weren't here to witness this.

∞

Danielle and Kennedy rushed to Mabel's side when she emerged from the office with tear-stained cheeks.

Kennedy asked, "Aunt Mabel, are you okay? What's wrong with Mike?"

Danielle looked toward the door. "I'll go see about him."

Mabel held Danielle back. "No. He needs some time to process and cool down."

Danielle hesitated, but something about Mabel's touch sent her heart into overdrive. "Why? What happened?"

Thaddeus' voice broke through the foyer before Mabel could answer.

"Well, family, it seems I'm the proud papa of a thirty-seven-year-old son."

Audible gasps escaped everyone, and the room quieted.

A reporter entered the building, but Jeffrey McCall, owner of McCall Resorts, rushed toward the entrance and escorted him out. "We're gonna need a moment." He turned his attention back to his brother. "What's going on?"

All eyes darted toward Mabel. "Thaddeus is Mike's father."

Danielle clutched her chest and glanced toward the door. Every fiber in her screamed to go after Mike. Though their relationship ended over five years ago, she clearly recalled how he adored Victor Stewart, the man he grew up believing was his father. He died when Mike was twenty-five, so he'd experienced and lost a father, but to know that he'd been slighted from knowing his biological father…Danielle knew Mike must have been a wreck.

Danielle looked at Kennedy. Her lips quivered, and she seemed to fight back emotions of her own. She was poised to go after Mike, but Danielle stopped her.

"I'll go. You stay with Mabel."

Mike took his relationships seriously—his seriousness had been one reason she'd ended their relationship five years ago. Though they were on great terms, it was too much for her. She wasn't ready to commit to anyone long-term, especially when she'd just lost her own father to brain cancer and her mother's osteoarthritis worsened and had consumed her. She couldn't maintain a healthy relationship with him and deal with her parents' illness. Letting him go seemed right five years ago, but one look at him today reminded her of the biggest mistake she'd made.

His eyes still held that same tenderness for her, but when he walked out of that room with Mabel and Thaddeus a while ago, that tenderness had been replaced with emptiness and helplessness.

She had to get to him.

Danielle whipped out her phone from her purse, pulled up Mike's contact information, and showed the screen to Kennedy. "Is this still Mike's number?"

"Yes."

Danielle tapped the call icon. She left Kennedy and Mabel's side and went to Nina. "Nina, I'm sorry, but I need to check on Mike after all of this. Do you need me to do anything?"

"No, ma'am. You're off duty. Check in on him and call me later." Nina hugged her. "Glad you stopped by. You'll just have to get your tour later."

"Sure thing. Love you, sis." Although, she'd been Nina's assistant for the past eight years, Nina was like a sister to her, but right now, Mike was at the forefront of her mind.

"Love you, too."

Danielle walked as fast as she could without sprinting out of the building and tried Mike's cell phone. No answer.

Okay, I know you're upset, but I need you to pick up.

She tried again. Still nothing.

After a few minutes, sirens wailed in the distance, and her heart and mind went into overdrive; her stomach somersaulted. Though the possibility of the sirens having something to do with Mike were remote, the flashing lights in the distance didn't bring her any comfort, especially when they were on the resort property.

Mike not answering his phone didn't help matters.

She glanced in the direction of the emergency alarms then locked eyes with one of the news reporters whose phone was hoisted between her ear and shoulder. She studied Danielle like she was the subject of conversation. A shiver washed over her. Was the news reporter giving her a warning? Whatever it was, Danielle had to see for herself.

Her legs had turned into mush, but somehow they carried her to her car. She hopped inside and drove in the direction of the emergency vehicles. About a mile and a half from the resort's main office, Danielle slowed her vehicle to a stop. An ambulance, fire truck, three police cars, resort security, and news station vans all blocked her view of the crash site. She jumped out of the car and maneuvered as close as she could to the accident.

"Ma'am, ma'am." An officer grabbed her arm and stilled her steps. "You can't go over there."

Danielle looked at the motionless body on the cement. She had to use everything in her power to get to him, so she lied. "Sir, that's my fiancé. Please, I need to get to him."

The officer's grip loosened, and Danielle took that as her opportunity to dash away. Even her four-inch pumps couldn't stop her from getting to Mike. She kneeled at his side, lifting his bloody hand to her chest.

"Please, baby, you have to pull through. There are so many things I never got the chance to tell you. Please, Mike." She rested his bloody hand over her thrashing heart, not caring that the stain may not come out. "Can you feel that? I still love you."

The officer was back at her side. "Ma'am, please let EMS do what they need to do to get him to Memorial Hermann."

Danielle stepped back. Her hands trembled. She stuffed them under her arms to still the shaking. When that didn't help, she shoved her hands into her pockets.

What am I doing?

Danielle whipped out her phone and called Kennedy.

"Kennedy…It's an emergency…It's Mike…Yes, I'm sure. Meet me at Memorial Hermann…I'm following the ambulance."

TWO

The what-if thoughts plowed through Danielle's mind.

What if Mike suffered permanent damage from the accident?

What if he didn't make it through surgery?

What if he blamed Mabel for his injuries?

She contorted her face to ease the throbbing headache while she paced in the emergency waiting room. Danielle had been inside the hospital so many times with her parents, and then Nina, over the past few years that all she needed was a pair of scrubs and she'd be right at home, except nothing about this place comforted her or gave her any peace like home.

When she heard Kennedy call her name, she spun on her heels. Danielle fought to contain her tears, swallowing the aching that rose in her throat. She needed to reassure them that everything would be okay, though she didn't have that assurance herself. Someone needed to be strong until they received any news. She gripped Mabel in a firm embrace first, followed by Kennedy.

Danielle fought to keep her voice calm. "I don't have any news yet. Still waiting."

Mabel sobbed. "It's my fault. I shouldn't have let him leave like that. I should've told him the truth a long time ago. I should've—"

"Don't," Kennedy interjected.

Thaddeus stormed inside the emergency room, his chest heaving and worry lines deep enough in his forehead to form pockets. He stalked over to the check-in station and flaunted his credentials. "I'm Dr. Thaddeus McCall, chief oncologist at Emory University Hospital Midtown in Atlanta. I need to know Mike Stewart's status—now. Who's the doctor? Is Mike in surgery?"

Maybe he thought being a doctor would get him more information than the check-in nurse had already given Danielle, which was nothing, but the check-in nurse wasn't impressed. Not a smile. Not compassionate eyes. Nothing changed in her features. Tight lips. Blank expression. "Sir, we'll call you when we have an update."

The rest of the McCall family filed inside the waiting room with the same questions.

What caused the accident?

Was Mike going to be okay?

Thaddeus turned to speak with the McCall family before the group joined Danielle, Kennedy, and Mabel's huddle.

"Let's pray for Mike," Mabel offered.

The group nodded in agreement and linked hands.

Mabel opened the prayer, but only gave a few words. Kennedy picked up where she left off and concluded the prayer. After the echo of Amens, Thaddeus pulled Mabel into his arms. Her tears stained his shirt. Though they hadn't seen each other in thirty-eight years, their bond was obvious, and Danielle found it hard to look away. She closed her eyes and whispered another prayer for Mike's health.

She'd do anything for him to recover so that he could get to know his father and see the way Thaddeus still loved

Mabel. He didn't say it, but it was evident in the way he held her.

Mike had once held her that way, too.

Darius McCall came to Kennedy's side and engulfed her in a bear hug. Nina and Andrew were engrossed in Andrew Jr., and Jeffrey and Rose McCall were wrapped up in conversation. Though in a room filled with others, Danielle was left alone with thoughts and memories she had of her and Mike and the two Christmases they'd spent with each other. She pulled out her phone and almost dropped it because of her trembling fingers. Danielle opened her photo app to view pictures of them together—pictures she should have discarded after all this time.

Mike had talked her into going on a hayride, which she didn't recall being comfortable, but he'd brought up their future together. Marriage. Children. Maybe even a pet, something she could do without. She sniffed, an act that caught Kennedy's attention, but Danielle waved her off. This would all be over soon. Mike would recover. She could move on and finish at Texas Southern University's Thurgood Marshall School of Law.

Nina broke her reverie. "Dani, let's go get some fresh air."

She looked to Kennedy who nodded and encouraged her to take a break. "I promise to come outside to get you if we hear anything."

Danielle blew a shaky breath, stood, and switched her phone to ring before she took Nina's arm and walked toward the exit. She turned for one last look toward the admissions area to ensure a doctor or nurse wasn't appearing with news of Mike's condition. It had been at least three hours. Why didn't it feel like they were treating Mike's situation like an emergency?

Danielle held on to Nina's arm, and for a while, they walked in silence.

Danielle was the first to speak. "Baby Drew is making you strong, honey. I think I feel your biceps."

Nina and Danielle burst into laughter.

"You can say something like that. I guess that's what happens when you carry twenty pounds around all day."

"I'm so happy for you. Life just seems to always work in your favor."

Nina stopped. "Are you kidding me? Remember where we were last year? It was me you were in the hospital with a little over a year ago."

"And look at you now. You're living your best life with the love of your life with a beautiful son to boot. Not to mention you practically live in paradise."

"Dani, don't do that. You're like a sister to me, and I've always encouraged you to go after your dreams. Now you're doing that. Pretty soon, you'll be my lawyer. I'll need to find another assistant."

"Maybe." Danielle inhaled and exhaled a long, slow breath. "But you're in a new phase in life now. You sort of have a new purpose. Your speeches will take a different turn now, and I'm pretty sure this new book is going to blow up."

"I wish you could see just how awesome you are, Dani. That's always been my prayer for you."

"And I know you believe that."

"Because it's true. You have to know that everything you've been through will only push you into becoming your greater self. You've got this. And no degree will change the gem that God has placed in you as a person, but," Nina said, squeezing her hand, "I'm rooting for you, sis."

"I'm gonna make us both proud."

Nina wrapped her arms around Danielle's neck. She pulled away after a minute. They picked up their stride. "So, what's the deal with you and Mike? Is something going on I didn't know about between you two?"

"No." Part of her regretted that truth. Her chest burned as the word left her lips. "I haven't seen or talked to him since the breakup. It was so nice to see him today. I just wish the evening didn't end like this, you know? Makes me think about all the things I should've said or done before now."

"And that makes me wonder about what really happened between you two. One minute you were doing fine, and the next it was over. What happened anyway? I thought you guys were happy together."

Danielle slowed her pace. Her mind traveled back to the days she and Mike were a couple. Nina's assessment was accurate. She and Mike were happy.

She released a heavy breath. "Things were good between us, but when my Dad died and then my mom became sick, it was all too much. Around that same time, Mike proposed. Remember?"

Nina nodded.

"I'd accepted his proposal, but ended up giving the ring back. Everything I was going through became too much—didn't want to bring that negative energy into the relationship. I was down all the time. My heart was just heavy. Mike understood and tried to cheer me up, but I guess I slowly pulled away. Didn't answer his calls as much. Dates became less frequent. In the end, we—well, I—decided we should take a break for a while."

"And by a while you mean…?"

"We never reconnected. And I admit, it's all on me. I messed up. But as time went on, I decided it was best to just let things stay as they were. Honestly, that's probably the biggest mistake I ever made."

Danielle's voice lowered and she added, "My biggest regret."

"Dani, this may be your opportunity to right your wrong. When Mike comes out of this, I think you should tell him how you feel. It's obvious you still love him. And we know he'll be okay. We all believe that."

"Deep down, I know that to be true, too. And knowing that I've never loved anyone like I've loved him, this crisis helped me realize I want the chance to try with him again. I guess I can say your situation with Andrew inspires me, too, but I'm not sure if he wants the same. Still, I'd rather tell him than to wonder."

"From your lips to God's ears."

Danielle chuckled. "You know I don't like it when you say that."

"Why? Because it's true? Honey, you've just spoken that into existence. I wouldn't be surprised if you got the chance to make good on your word, and if I were you, I wouldn't be concerned with whether he wants the same thing. His face lit up when he found out you were coming."

Nina's voice held a hint of something that made Danielle slip into fairytale-like thoughts. Danielle's heart galloped at the idea of Mike being excited to see her. Though when she thought back to the moment he took her hand inside the McCall Resorts office building and gazed into her eyes, she assumed his feelings hadn't changed. But who's to say she wasn't imagining things because of her own heart's desire?

And what about Brandon?

The fact she was at the hospital and not headed to his house for dinner complicated her relationship with him. Would Brandon understand her need to be there for her friend, even though he was her ex?

"That's nice and all, but we both know you can sport a pair of rose-colored glasses when it comes to relationships."

"Maybe," Nina said slowly, "but how do you think Kennedy and D got together? My rose-colored glasses work, honey." Nina winked. "I can sense these sorts of things, I guess. Momma Rose can, too."

Danielle knew all about Nina and her mother-in-law, Rose McCall's, conspiracy to help Darius McCall and Kennedy get together. Cute story, but life didn't work out that way for everyone.

Nina had this way of being certain and confident about most things life threw at her. Sometimes, Danielle wished she had a bit of Nina's strength. It was one of the reasons she enjoyed working as her assistant. Positivity and confidence oozed from Nina.

Danielle whispered another prayer for Mike's recovery.

Her phone rang, and Nina's phone chirped. They checked their devices simultaneously.

"Mike," they said in unison.

Danielle answered Kennedy's call and listened attentively to the details. She and Nina spun on their heels and speed-walked back into the emergency waiting room.

Stay calm.

Her heart didn't listen. If it had the power, it would have popped out of her chest and raced her back inside the hospital.

They made it in enough time to listen to the doctor explain Mike's injuries. Mabel buried her head against Thaddeus' chest while he attempted to comfort her by rubbing his palm along her back. Everyone else shared the same expression. Wide eyes. Open mouths.

"Mike came through surgery just fine. He had a broken arm, which we realigned during surgery. We gave him blood for the loss he sustained after the accident." He took a deep breath, and Danielle's stomach clenched to brace herself for the bad news. "Mike also suffered an intracranial injury. We won't know the impact until he wakes up, but we believe he may suffer memory loss. It could be loss of memory from events just prior to the accident or selective amnesia where he may not have memory of events from certain periods of time."

Mabel inched forward. Her prayer hands clutched at her chest. "When will I be able to see him?"

"You may see him now, but only one person in the room at a time."

Mabel, Kennedy, Thaddeus, and Danielle followed the doctor so they could take turns seeing Mike.

Danielle sat outside his door while his family did their rounds of visiting. Mabel went first, then Kennedy.

Memory loss? Selective amnesia?

How would she even address him? Would he even know who she was? And equally worse, would he have to learn a second time that Thaddeus was his biological father?

Danielle leaned forward in her seat and hugged her waist. The posture didn't stop the topsy-turvy movement of her stomach. She fought back tears—tears that could be the mourning of the Mike she once knew and who once knew her. He might wake up and she'd be a total stranger.

She couldn't handle the thought.

Danielle leaped out of her seat and paced the floor.

The all-too-familiar scent of disinfectant burned her nostrils.

The chatter of the nurses passing by made her cringe.

The tiny hairs on her skin suddenly pricked her.

All those years apart haunted her thoughts. Why didn't she just pick up the phone and call him at least four years ago? Even one year ago would have been better than witnessing him like this with the idea that he may not recognize her.

Okay, I'm freaking out for nothing. Everything will be fine. Mike will remember me.

She wasn't sure how long she'd been waiting on the other side of that door when Kennedy walked out. She held on to the doorknob and locked eyes with Danielle.

"He's awake now."

Mabel and Thaddeus both jumped out of their seats, but Kennedy shook her head.

"He's asking for Danielle."

THREE

Every muscle in Mike's body ached.

The doctor mentioned something about him being in a car accident, and he felt every twinge of pain. Despite the pain, all he wanted was to see his fiancée, Danielle. Laying eyes on her always lifted his spirits. Besides, other than his mother, he didn't know any other woman who cared for him and loved him as much as Danielle did.

He winced at the pain shooting up the left side of his abdomen. The door creaked open, and he attempted to shift himself in the bed at the sound of her voice. But his pain wouldn't allow his body to be in any other position than his back.

"Mike."

She linked her fingers with his. He squeezed her hand with as much strength as he could muster.

"Babe, you don't know how happy it makes me to know that you're here by my side. The Lord smiled down on me when he gave me you as my future wife. I can't wait to marry you."

Danielle tensed.

Had he said something wrong?

Mike glanced down at her bare ring finger.

"Babe, what happened? Why aren't you wearing your ring?"

The confusion in her wrinkled eyebrows and forehead sent alarms through his already banged-up core. He didn't have it in him to worry about a ring right now, so he dropped the subject. All that mattered was that Danielle stood at his bedside when he needed her most.

"How are you feeling? Crazy question, I know." She rested her free palm across his forehead like she was taking his temperature, then she caressed his low fade before pulling back.

"Much better after that." He attempted to shift himself to a more upright position. "But to answer your question, everything hurts."

She locked eyes with him for a moment and chewed the corner of her bottom lip—the same thing she always did when trying to decide whether to share something important.

Danielle released a pent-up breath and massaged his knuckles. "Well, that's expected. You were hit hard enough for them to find you lying in the middle of the street. You'll likely be on painkillers for a while."

"As long as I have you with me, I'll pull through alright."

"Mike…" Danielle paused and did that thing with her eyes and bottom lip again. "What's the last thing you remember?"

"Ah, things are fuzzy, but I remember us taking the hayride in Rosenburg and us planning our future. Dinner at Eddie V's. The proposal. You agreeing to marry me. Dropping you off at home."

"I see."

"Wait." Mike studied her intently for a moment. "How long have I been out? You've changed your hair. The light color is beautiful."

Danielle fingered her long tresses. "Thank you."

"You've always been the most beautiful woman in the world in my eyes."

Danielle blinked back tears. He couldn't figure out why she'd become so emotional. Was it because he'd been bruised and banged up?

He parted his lips to ask, but the doctor entered the room. "How's our patient?"

He removed the stethoscope and placed it across several places on Mike's chest.

Satisfied with Mike's heart activity, he hung the stethoscope around his neck and asked Mike questions about his memory. Mike shared his engagement with Danielle. The doctor looked from Mike to Danielle and down to her bare ring finger. He probably wondered why she wasn't wearing his ring, just as Mike had.

With Every Moment

"Sweetheart, I think your mom would like to be by your side while the doctor discusses your injuries. I'll just be right outside the door."

Mike squeezed her hand and nodded. The last thing he wanted was for her to leave. Seeing her right now somehow made him feel like that was the first time they'd been with each other in years. Whatever the case, he didn't like the emptiness that lingered when she disappeared on the other side of the door.

Both Mike and the doctor turned their attention Mabel, who walked in the room accompanied by a man who appeared vaguely familiar. Who was this man, and why was he displaying such affection toward his mother? His hands securely gripping her arms and guiding her through the door like a fragile piece of china seemed a bit much, especially for someone he didn't know she had in her life. Come to think of it, she hadn't been seriously involved with anyone since his father, Victor, died seven years ago.

That saying that it took more muscles to frown than to smile had to be true. Mike's face ached from the displeasure in his features.

He tilted his head toward the man who towered over his mom by at least a foot. "Mom, who's this?"

She glanced up toward the man wearing an expression that Mike couldn't quite read before she turned her attention toward the doctor.

"We can talk about it later. Let's hear what the doctor has to say."

She made herself comfortable on the side of his bed and took his hand. The man hadn't said anything. He only nodded and took a nearby seat. Mike cut his eyes toward him, and their eyes locked. He couldn't help but sense the familiarity, but couldn't figure out how he knew him.

"It seems that Mike is experiencing selective amnesia caused by the intracranial injury. This type of amnesia is associated when someone forgets certain parts of their memory. It could be blocking certain parts of traumatic events. Forgetting relationships. Forgetting certain time periods. After speaking with him and Miss Adams, this seems to be some, but not all, events over the past five years."

"What? How do you figure that?" Even his elevated voice pained his chest.

The doctor hit the side key to illuminate his iPad. He scrolled through images of Mike's scans to show how the impact of the crash affected him.

"So what am I supposed to do, doc? How am I supposed to live my life knowing that part of it is missing?"

"With the help of your family, I believe we'll see positive results."

Mike pressed his head back into the pillow and squeezed his eyes shut.

Surely this has to be a mistake.

He clenched his fists by his sides, like that would help bring back memories he didn't even know he'd lost. What did that mean for his relationship with Danielle or any of his life?

Five years?

He couldn't wrap his head around the idea of not remembering the last five years of his life.

Mike lashed out, not caring that his chest and throat pained him when he raised his voice. "Is that why I don't know who this guy is?" He pointed at the man whose head shot up. He locked eyes with Mike, but didn't respond. There was something almost familiar about him, yet Mike couldn't recall ever seeing this man in his entire life.

"Why can't he keep his hands off you?"

The man's features remained unchanged. He couldn't describe the look in his eyes. Not pity. Something else—something he didn't care to think about right now.

There were more important things to deal with, like the fact a chunk of his life was missing, and he didn't have any idea how to piece it back together again.

Mabel didn't answer his question. Instead, she covered Mike's hand with her palm and addressed the physician. "Doctor, will he ever regain his memory? What can we do to help him?"

"Let's remain hopeful. I've seen this go both ways. The best thing you can do for him is to be patient. Help him continue his normal routine. Work. Exercise. Time with family…Whatever he did before the accident. It's important that he's surrounded by loved ones who can help trigger important memories, but don't push."

"I see."

Mike stared straight ahead. What did any of this mean for his life? Not only was a strange man at his bedside, but what about his relationship with Danielle? Did she even still love him the way he loved her? Moisture threatened to increase in his eyes.

Was he living his life without her?

That couldn't be true.

They were created to be together.

There was no way they'd be apart.

But a separation could explain why she wasn't wearing her ring. Had they married and divorced? Mike dismissed the silly thought. He concluded she wouldn't be there if they were divorced. Mike fought to recall an inkling of a memory. What was he supposed to do with his life knowing that he'd lost a portion of it because of a brain injury?

He may as well have been bulldozed because the ache in his head and chest caused a similar heap of pain.

One thing that brought him a shred of hope was that Danielle still looked at him the way he remembered. Her

43

eyes encouraged him in a way that made him believe he could run a mile in his condition, although bruised with a few broken parts. And she'd be there at the end. But there was also sadness. Could it be because of the state his body was in?

"Danielle. I can recover with Danielle by my side."

"But son, I—"

The man stood and interrupted her. "Mabel, I'll go get Danielle. If she's the key to helping Mike recover even a portion of his memory, we need to ensure she's around to help. I think that's what's best."

The doctor nodded in what Mike believed to be concurrence with his mom's man friend. "I'll come back in to check on you in a bit, Mr. Stewart."

Who was that man? And what was it about him that melted his mother's resolve and had her looking at him with love-struck eyes?

∞

Danielle paced outside of Mike's room trying to wrap her mind around Thaddeus' request. Her legs became more and more like gelatin with each step.

44

"When you say stick around, what exactly do you mean by that?" Danielle asked.

"I mean Mike believes you're his fiancée, so I want you to be his fiancée until he regains his memory," Thaddeus explained. Something told her he wasn't used to the word *no*.

She wanted Mike to recover just as much as his family, but to go to such great lengths to do so was out of her comfort zone. And absolute ridiculousness.

"And what if he doesn't?"

"We have to err on the side of hope and faith."

"I don't think it works like that. What's going to happen when he realizes I was only pretending to be his fiancée? At some point, he's gonna expect me to walk down that aisle."

"Listen, Danielle, I know this is asking a lot of you, but we want Mike to regain his memory. Right now, he doesn't know where to turn or what to think. For him, you are his constant."

"And is this your professional opinion, Dr. McCall, that I should pretend to be someone I'm not?"

Thaddeus blew a stream of air and turned away from her. He ran his hand over his shiny bald head where she could see tiny gray hairs threatening to make their reappearance. He faced Danielle again.

"Do you love him?"

"My love for him doesn't make a difference."

"Actually, it makes all the difference. I believe your love for him will aid in his healing."

Danielle sat in a chair outside of Mike's room, leaned forward, and hugged her elbows. None of this was supposed to happen. Her plan had been to see Mike today and catch up on old times. They'd missed out on their chance to be permanent fixtures in each other's lives.

She rocked. Her thoughts moved as quickly as the back-and-forth motion of her body.

"I have a boyfriend. Am I just supposed to end that relationship?"

"Is it serious?"

"That's beside the point."

"Is it? Do you love him like you love Mike?"

"No, but Mike and I haven't been together in over five years. I can't just slip back into the role of happy girlfriend—well according to him, fiancée. It's insane to even consider. Besides, I have so much other stuff going on in my life right now. I'm a student in Thurgood Marshall's School of Law. Next month starts my last semester to finish my J.D. This whole setup sounds like a distraction."

Danielle could sense his wheels turning. His eyes lit up, and he wagged his finger like he was conjuring up an idea. "If you don't mind my asking, how are you paying for law school?"

"I'm applying for Student loans this semester, why?"

"What if I offer to pay your tuition?"

No student loans. She could graduate debt free. Up until this point, she'd paid for law school with scholarships and money she'd saved. If Thaddeus paid her tuition for her final semester, that would also free up additional money for her to help her mom.

But that arrangement had wrong written all over it.

She didn't need money to be a part of Mike's life.

But it won't hurt.

"I can't take your money, Dr. McCall." *But you need his money.*

"What else can I do to help make this decision easier for you? Listen," he said, holding her shoulders and boring his gaze into hers. It wasn't until that moment that she realized he and Mike had the same eyes—eyes that could nearly convince her to do almost anything, except marry Mike. "I want to have a relationship with my son. I need him to feel as much like himself and gain as much of his memory as he possibly can."

"What's stopping you from doing that now?"

"You."

Danielle inhaled a sharp breath. So sharp that a pain shot through the center of her chest.

"What do you mean me?" She didn't know whether she should be offended.

"Like I said, to him, you're what he believes to be the only constant in his life. If he finds out you two aren't engaged, I think it'll tear him apart. Learning that I'm his biological father won't help the situation. I think it may push him farther away from me and his mother, and I'd never want to do anything to hurt either of them."

Danielle folded her arms across her chest and squared her shoulders. "It seems this arrangement is helping you more than anyone else."

"I'd like to help you in any way I can. Tell me what I can do for you, and I'll do it."

Pay Mom's medical bills for the next year and cover law school.

The mere thought made her feel dirty, but he'd offered, hadn't he? It wasn't like it was her idea, but it would surely release the burden heaped on her shoulders if Thaddeus could stand by his word to do anything to help.

Danielle explained her mother's osteoarthritis and need for hip replacement surgery. With every word, she swallowed the discomfort that rose in her throat. Did this make her a conniving, dirty person? She and Thaddeus were practically family anyway, right, given that he was Mike's father and she'd be his daughter-in-law?

How would she explain this situation to any sane person? To Nina? To her boyfriend, Brandon?

No one had to know the whole truth.

"Done. Say no more," Thaddeus said after Danielle's explanation.

Danielle extended her hand, and Thaddeus engulfed it in a firm handshake. Her stomach weaved itself into a knot at the thought of what she'd agreed to do.

FOUR

Was she doing the right thing by pretending to be Mike's fiancée?

Was it really in his best interest to believe that they'd stayed together all this time?

Danielle rang Brandon's doorbell and fidgeted with her keys while she waited for him to answer. Knowing what she was about to do, it didn't seem right to use the key he'd given her last month.

Brandon opened the door with a smile that didn't reach his eyes. Did he know what she was about to do?

"Sorry about missing dinner last night," she offered.

"Don't worry about it. Come on in."

He moved to allow her inside. She walked in, but didn't walk into the living area as she normally would have.

Instead, she stopped in the foyer and turned to face him when he closed the door.

Danielle fidgeted with the keys again. "I have something to tell you, and I don't really know how to say it."

"You can tell me anything. Haven't I always made it easy for you to share your thoughts with me?"

He stepped closer, but Danielle inched back and shook her head. She needed to see his face when she told him what she'd agreed to do for Mike. Brandon frowned and disappointment laced his eyes. See, she'd already hurt his feelings and hadn't revealed her truth yet.

You don't know how he's gonna respond.

"Remember the friend I mentioned was in a car accident yesterday?"

Brandon nodded. His eyebrows bunched together in a way that made her heart sick. *Ugh.* She hated to be the person to put him in this situation, especially since he'd been so good to her.

"That friend is Mike Stewart, a guy I dated over five years ago. He suffered a brain injury and doesn't remember much of what's happened over the last five years."

"Go, on," Brandon said when Danielle hesitated.

This doesn't even make sense to me. I know Brandon won't understand.

"He thinks I'm his fiancée."

"I'm sorry to hear that. How did he handle it when you told him you were in a relationship with me?"

Danielle shifted her gaze to the keys in her hand. She'd already removed his key from the ring. There was no way he'd let her keep it after she told the entire story.

"I didn't correct him. None of us did. We agreed—"

"Hold on. What? Why not? You can't seriously allow a man to think you're about to marry him when you're in a relationship with—"

"I know it sounds crazy, Brandon, but his family and I think it'll help with his recovery if—"

"And just what am I supposed to do while you're out pretending to be someone else's fiancée? At any point, did you think about me and our relationship when you made this decision? We were talking about meeting each other's parents. Is he the reason you've been stalling our relationship?"

"How can you say that? I haven't seen or talked to him in over five years."

"And yet, you jump at the opportunity to fake an engagement to him?"

"I'm sorry, Brandon. I know this is crazy, and I don't expect you to understand." *I hardly understand, but I feel like I have to do this.*

Tears filled her eyes. She fought hard to keep them at bay, but lost control when she saw the water in his eyes. She hated to do this to him.

Danielle handed Brandon his key. He accepted it and pulled her into his arms for what she knew to be the last time. She squeezed. Hard.

"I'm sorry, Brandon." Her voice was muffled against his chest.

"Me, too. I just wish you loved me more than you love him. Take care of yourself, Danielle."

Danielle eased out of his embrace and walked out of the door. She didn't turn around to look at him. She couldn't knowing that she was the reason behind the pain in his eyes.

With Every Moment

She climbed into her car and backed out of his driveway, navigating through the Houston traffic to get back to Mike's side at Memorial Hermann Cypress Hospital. She glanced over at what she remembered to be Mike's favorite treats, riding shotgun. Peppermint chocolate chip cookies. Would those help jar his memory? He ate them almost daily during the two Christmas seasons they'd spent together. They weren't her favorite, but they'd grown on her. In the past five years, she usually enjoyed one during the season. Munching on the cookies always brought about thoughts of him.

Traffic halted, and she stole another glance.

What was she thinking anyway? Agreeing to Thaddeus' arrangement? She didn't have the nerve to tell Nina just yet. Brandon didn't understand what she was doing for the McCall family. Shoot, she didn't fully understand it.

So, why are you doing it?

But she loved Mike, even as a friend, and what kind of friend would she be if she didn't help just a little, especially considering his family seemed to think that she was the key to unlocking his memory?

But she couldn't do this forever. There had to be a deadline. Maybe six months? She had to do her research. If Mike didn't regain his memory in six months, then perhaps it wasn't coming back, then she could end this farce.

Long enough for you to get what you want out of it?

Why did her conscious want to show up now?

Danielle ground her teeth, wearing them down with worry. *Think. I'll be finishing law school soon. Surely I can work up an argument to plead my case.*

Her biggest concern in all of this was Mike regaining his memory and believing she deceived him to get what she wanted. Would he believe that this was her way of helping him?

Her phone rang. Nina. Surely, she knew what was going on by now. No sense in avoiding her. Maybe Nina could talk some sense into her—confirm she was losing her mind and to quit while she was ahead.

"Fiancée?"

"I expected a 'hey, how're you doing, lady?' first." Danielle sighed. "So, I guess Thaddeus broke the news."

"He did. Honestly, I was quite shocked. I didn't think you'd go along with it."

"I can't believe I'm going along with it. This could turn out bad. Like, what if Mike regains his memory, and he thinks I was running some scheme just to get Thaddeus' money? Or what if he never gets his memory back? At some point, he's gonna expect me to walk down the aisle. Breaking up from a fake engagement is going to be just as hard as breaking off a real one."

"Or…" Nina spoke slowly. Danielle could tell that she was coming up with something that was even crazier. She'd been around Nina long enough to know when that was happening. Her body warned her as much each time, like now. The tiny hairs on her arms stood.

Traffic opened up, and Danielle relaxed a bit, but was still on high alert because of whatever Nina's mind was formulating.

"Whatever you're thinking, stop thinking it."

"Listen. Hear me out. What if this is just what you and Mike need to realize you're meant to be together?

Maybe you won't have to break anything off when you recognize it."

"I don't know about that, but I'll go on record saying that I'm doing this for him. It's not about Thaddeus paying for my tuition or my mom's medical bills."

"You don't have to explain to me. I saw the way you looked at him—we all did. I don't think Uncle Thad would've asked this of you if he doubted your feelings. It'll all work out, even if there's a little turbulence along the way."

Nina gave motivational speeches for a living, so Danielle didn't expect anything less from her.

"Thanks, sis."

Danielle talked with Nina for several more minutes before ending the call.

Her mom had always told her if she didn't have any peace about a situation not to move forward, and pretending to be Mike's fiancée didn't give her any peace. She'd take a box of his favorite cookies to him and break the news after he'd eaten a few. But she would hang around for the next few months and aid in his recovery in whatever way she could—just not as his fiancée.

Student loans could easily cover tuition expenses. And maybe she could see about getting a payment plan to take care of her mom's medical expenses. She could take care of everything without Thad's help. Danielle arrived at Memorial Hermann Cypress and whipped her car into a parking space.

Yes, that's what she'd do.

On cue, her phone rang when she shifted the gear into park. Her instinct was to ignore the call until she saw her mom's number glowing on the screen.

"Hey, mom."

"Hey, sugar. What time are you picking me up for our little Christmas shindig later this week?"

Danielle ground her teeth. How could she have forgotten about making Christmas dinner and hanging out with her own mother? This thing with Mike had knocked her off her center. She had to be there for him, even as his friend. She was moments away from telling him the truth about their relationship.

Her mother groaned. The sound ripped through Danielle's heart. It seemed her osteoarthritis caused her more and more pain.

"You okay, mom?"

"Yeah. It's just this old hip bothering me. I'm alright. Don't change the subject. Are you trying to skip out on Christmas dinner?"

"I've got that taken care of, but there might be a few changes. We may have a visitor, but I'll let you know for sure later. I'm more worried about you than Christmas dinner. Are you sure you're okay? When is your next doctor's visit?"

"I'm not thinking about that doctor. Nothing he's done has helped this pain. Nothing. I've just learned to deal with it by doing my exercises and using this old brace when I need to." Her mother wore a hip brace to manage the pain from osteoarthritis. At first, she'd wear it once a week, but lately she wore it almost daily. The pain grew worse and worse, and Danielle's heart broke every time she had to see her mother limping and wincing from the discomfort.

"We may need to consider surgery. I hate to see you in so much pain."

"Dani, I don't want my medical issues to stress you out. I don't think Medicare will cover surgery anyhow."

"If finances weren't a factor, would you at least consider it?"

Bernadette huffed but didn't respond. Danielle had her answer, and she knew exactly what she had to do to ensure all would be well in her mother and Mike's world.

Stick with the plan.

"Alright. I love you, mom. I'm gonna run visit a friend. I'll call you later with the details for Christmas."

"Love you, too. Talk to you later."

Danielle ended the call and glanced toward the box of peppermint chocolate chip cookies that taunted her.

She couldn't back out of Thaddeus' plan. The truth would have to wait. Her mother needed more medical attention, and Thaddeus had become her best option to make that happen. And who knows? Maybe he could refer them to a doctor to receive better care. After all, Bernadette hadn't been too happy with her current physician.

Danielle checked her reflection in the sun visor mirror, grabbed the cookies from the passenger seat, and climbed out of the car. She marched inside the hospital and sucked in slow streams of air. She drowned out her conscience with each click of her heels against the tile flooring.

Mike's smile greeted her as soon as she opened his door.

Time to play fiancée.

FIVE

At the sight of Danielle entering his hospital room, Mike momentarily forgot the pain wracking his body. Her twinkling eyes had a way of making his emotional load seem lighter. Had it always been like that between them? He couldn't recall. All he knew and trusted were the raw emotions coursing through him.

"Good morning, babe. Guess what I have for you," Danielle half sang and jiggled a white gift box wrapped in green and red ribbon.

He waved her over.

"You know you're enough, but I'll take whatever you have in that box for me, too."

She handed the box to him, and he took a whiff.

"Don't tell me you went and bought Peppermint chocolate chip cookies. These have been my favorite since I was like seven."

Danielle leaned in and kissed his forehead. Mike closed his eyes and relished in the contact. She hadn't seemed to want to share any closeness with him before, which he chalked up to the fact that he was recovering from the accident and she was worried she'd inflict pain on him somehow. On a level of one to ten, today he measured the pain at a four. Perhaps he looked better, too, because something about her had changed. She seemed less worried.

"Yep. Thought these would put a smile on your face considering the circumstances."

Mike placed the box to his side and reached for Danielle's hands. "I can't say enough how much it means to me that you're here. I don't know what was going on with us before the accident, good or bad, but I appreciate you being selfless."

"I'd do anything for you. That has never changed."

He couldn't pin together where, when, or how, but his mind somehow remembered her saying those exact words to him. He scrunched his eyebrows to recall the memory, not realizing he'd squeezed Danielle's hand tight until she jerked it away from him.

"Sorry. I can't explain it, but it was as if my mind was trying to recall a memory, but I couldn't get to it. Almost like it was blocked or something. Crazy, right?"

Danielle shrugged. "I wouldn't call it crazy. A piece of you is missing, and it's quite natural to want it back. But no matter what, I'll be by your side."

"Speaking of by my side, had we picked a wedding date before my accident? That seems like something I'd never forget."

Danielle turned away from him to grab a chair and pulled it closer to his bedside. She sat. The slant in her eyes told him setting a wedding date worried her, but why?

"I really don't think we should talk about a wedding when you're lying in a hospital bed."

"That's exactly why I think we should. I almost lost my life, babe. Well, technically, I guess I lost some of it since there are some memories I don't have. All I know is that I want to spend whatever time I have left with you. I don't know what happened with us before the accident, but how would you feel right now if I weren't here? We can't allow small stuff to get in the way, you know? Seize the moment."

The corners of her lips turned upward.

"I'll tell you what. How about we talk through it more after Christmas?"

"You know I love Christmas, so I'm a little disappointed. You sure we didn't plan a Christmas wedding?"

Danielle tossed her head back and chuckled, but Mike didn't join in the laughter.

"Wait. You're serious? Christmas is only, what…six days from now? We hadn't planned a Christmas wedding and we wouldn't be able to pull anything together that fast now anyway."

"We've been engaged for five years. Why aren't we already married? And why aren't you wearing your ring?"

Danielle's smile faded. The light left her eyes. Her shoulders slumped. What did he say wrong?

She took his hand in hers and pressed her lips together before answering the questions that plagued him.

"I've been focusing on finishing law school and on my job with Nina. But let's not worry about any of that right now. I want you better, then we can concentrate on us. Promise."

"I guess I'll have to take that."

Danielle's answer didn't sit well with him. In fact, his head ached more while he attempted to sort through what she didn't say. Did she somehow think being with him was holding her back from work or school? Surely he'd been supportive this whole time, right?

"Thanks. You know it'd be hard for me to think about a wedding anyway when I'm so concerned about you."

"I understand. I guess I haven't really stopped to think about how hard it must be for you to see me like this."

"You hurt, I hurt, but the good news is that your family has been supportive, and with so many of us pulling for you and willing to do whatever it takes to help your recovery, I'm sure you'll get better sooner rather than later."

"I love you, Danielle Adams. I don't know what I did for God to bless me with you. It's probably nothing, just favor, but I'm thankful." He raised her hand to his lips and pressed a light kiss on the back of it.

"You lay it on thick, don't you?" Danielle chuckled. "I love you, too, Mike. Never stopped."

See, it was the way she said things that worried him. Like that—like they hadn't been together—but that couldn't be true because she wouldn't be sitting at his bedside, would she? And he simply couldn't imagine having spent any portion of the last five years of his life without her. He'd be a fool to let her go. She was the only woman who could make his heart do crazy things inside of his chest—the only woman he'd ever loved.

∞

Had Mike noticed he turned her into a nervous wreck the second he mentioned a wedding date? And why would he not bring up the subject when he believed they were engaged? She'd turned her back and focused on the nearest object, which had been the chair—a time-saving chair she used to mask her discomfort and stall the topic once more.

How long did Thaddeus think she could do this?

For goodness' sake, how long did she think she could do this?

Mike had the magic touch, though. Whenever their hands connected, it was as if they were meant to hold hands for the rest of their days.

As silly as it sounded, she'd say yes if he asked her to marry him, even after all the time they'd been apart. She was honest about one thing: She'd never stopped loving him.

"I'll be out of here in a few days. What's the plan for Christmas? I apologize for not knowing what the plans are. You know?" Mike pointed to his bandage-wrapped head.

"Oh, it's not your fault."

Another stall.

She complimented him on his strength through this situation while she searched for the right words to tell him about their nonexistent Christmas plans.

"I wouldn't worry about any plans we had. With the McCall resort finished, we could just stay there." *That's probably already on Thaddeus' agenda.*

Mike raised questioning eyebrows.

"McCall Resorts is a project SCI's construction team had been working on for nearly a year. You ran the project, and from what I heard, you were on top of your game."

Danielle stiffened. Had Mike caught her slip about what she *heard*? She rushed to add, "We were at the ribbon cutting ceremony for the grand opening before your accident."

She held her breath a moment, hoping he wouldn't delve deeper into what she *heard*. They were engaged. She should have firsthand knowledge of everything happening in his life.

Think like a fiancée.

"Considering I was a big part of this project, why did I leave such an important event? Did something happen?"

Danielle should not be the one explaining that he left the resort upset when he learned Thaddeus was his biological father. She couldn't lie either. Wasn't it enough she agreed to this fake engagement arrangement? She refused to stack her lies. The engagement lie was big enough.

His eyes pierced hers. Made her heart churn. She hated she'd allowed herself to be put in this predicament.

"I'm not really sure. I was talking with Nina, and you were having a conversation with your mom. You left without saying anything. I was worried, so I went to look for you after you didn't answer any of my calls. Shortly after, I found you lying in the street surrounded by EMTs."

There. Mabel could fill in the holes, mainly why he stormed out of the office.

Mike nodded. He scrunched his eyebrows so hard that Danielle thought they would connect.

Danielle covered his hand with hers. "I know this is hard, babe, but try not to wear yourself out trying to regain your memories. You have us all to help fill in the gaps. I'm sure your mom can explain what happened. Don't worry yourself too much about it."

"You know anything about the man who was with her?"

"How about we take a break from trying to piece puzzles together and talk about what you want me to give you as a Christmas present?"

Mike's lips curled into a smile.

Crisis averted.

"Since I have to wait for that wedding, I'll need some time to think about it, but honestly, as long as we can celebrate together, I'm all good."

He motioned with his index finger for her to move closer. He gave her a quick peck on the lips like that was something he did all the time—and in his mind, that probably was true. But for her, she should have known better.

Her breath caught.

Thoughts of all the shared kisses she'd experienced with him in the past clouded her mind. She closed her eyes and reminded herself that this was pretend.

Well, Mike had just made it real—and real wasn't part of the plan.

And just what did you think would happen?

She had that coming. There was no way he wouldn't want to lay random kisses on his fiancée every now and then.

She backed away, nearly tripping into her seat. There had to be a way to limit the closeness. What if he regained his memory and realized that he was actually with someone else? It's not like that wasn't possible. Or better yet, what if in his current life he'd completely gotten over her?

Mike's voice cut through her reverie. "And speaking of gifts, let's try these cookies."

With Every Moment

Danielle gladly accepted one and stuffed it into her mouth. At least for a few minutes, she could keep herself from saying something she didn't have any business saying.

There were three light taps on the door. Danielle turned to see Mabel and Thad coming in again. She rose from her seat, excused herself for a moment, and shot them her best we-need-to-talk look on her way out the door.

Her plan had been to help Mike without getting her heart overly involved, but that kiss, as small as it was, reminded her of everything she'd once had with him. She'd only just begun, and she wasn't sure how long she could keep this up.

SIX

Danielle paced the hall outside of Mike's hospital room. She wrung her fingers, rolled her shoulders, and tilted her head from side to side. What was she doing? Preparing for a boxing match? Every time she marched past his door, she glared as if she possessed Jedi powers to transport one of Mike's parents into the hallway to talk with her. Danielle gnawed at her bottom lip and mentally rehearsed the chaos coursing through her mind.

How did she expect this all to end?

Though unlikely, if Mike regained his memory tomorrow, could she move on with her life as if none of this happened?

Technically, nothing had happened yet, except she'd just broken up with her boyfriend and her emotions were all over the place. And that was enough.

With Every Moment

The door creaked open, and Thaddeus' frame filled the doorway. Danielle stopped pacing and turned to face him.

"I'm not sure how this is going to work. Mike is ready to get married—like now." Danielle folded her arms across her chest and jutted her chin. What was his plan to cure the wedding bells ringing in Mike's head?

Thaddeus heaved a deep breath and shoved his hands in his pockets. "So I've heard. He mentioned it a moment ago—said you two were going to make plans after Christmas."

"I'm not sure about that, but that's the answer I gave him so we could table the discussion for now. Though I love him, marriage is serious business and is not part of the plan. I can't deceive him like that. I think you should at least tell him who you are. He has questions about you, too. There's just too much he doesn't know, and I can't help but feel like none of this will end well if we keep this up. Something's gotta give."

"I understand that, but I also know that we can't rush this process and that we shouldn't throw too much at him at once. We'll tell him about me, but after Christmas. In the meantime, I understand tuition is due for next semester."

He removed a folded envelope from his back pocket and handed it to her.

Danielle opened it to find a check that covered her tuition balance, her mother's medical care, plus extras.

She should be grateful and say thanks, but it all felt wrong.

Thaddeus must have read her mind because he added, "Just as we agreed. You take care of Mike, and I'll take care of you. If there's anything else you need, don't hesitate to ask. We simply want to do whatever we can to facilitate Mike's healing, and you seem to be the key."

"Thanks for staying true to you word, but let me go on record by saying that I'm doing this because I love Mike, not for your money."

Then why are you still holding the check?

"And I care about his well-being just as much as anyone else."

Thaddeus stepped closer. His eyes dropped from her head to her feet before he locked eyes with her. "I'm not questioning your feelings for Mike. Besides, Nina has had nothing but good things to say about you. I wouldn't ask this of you if I thought your heart wasn't in the right place. And judging by the way Mike looks at you, I know we're not making a mistake. I'm not privy to the facts of your past relationship with him, but I am certain of one thing."

"And what's that?"

"He loves you."

Thaddeus jammed his thumb toward Mike's room. "And he'd do the same thing for you if you were in that bed instead of him."

Air trapped in her chest.

Danielle closed her eyes and released a steady breath. Mike would do the same for her, even if he didn't feel the same way he did five years ago. He was loyal like that. He'd do everything within his power to help her heal.

"You're right. So what's the plan?"

Her stomach somersaulted when the words left her lips. Though she was pretending to be Mike's fiancée for the greater good, why did it feel so wrong?

Lord, please don't let this plan backfire and become something I later regret.

"Mabel and I will sit down to talk with him day after Christmas. I think it's best if you're there for the conversation. When he learned the truth last time, it didn't go well."

Danielle nodded. "I can be there."

The door creaked, and Mabel appeared. Her eyes weren't red today. Her smile had returned. Inching toward Danielle and Thaddeus was the woman she knew years prior.

Mabel hugged Danielle. When she released her, she clasped her hands and held them against her chest.

"Whatever you're doing is working. It does my heart some good to see Mike taking this in stride. Yes, he has some hurdles to cross, but he's hopeful."

"I don't think I'm doing much at all, really. Just being here for him. I think this relationship he believes we have is comforting him."

"Don't sell yourself short. Though your relationship isn't everything that he thinks it is, it's enough to get him through these horrible circumstances. I'm so thankful he has you."

Danielle nodded and switched the subject back to Thaddeus' identity.

"Mabel, I was just telling Thad how important it is for Mike to know his relationship to him. Mike has a lot of questions. He's so confused right now. I just think it's best that we tell him one truth to ease his worries. Thad and I agreed that he'd tell him after Christmas."

Mabel's smile faded, and Danielle's belly dropped.

Oh, no.

"Are you in agreement with us?"

Thaddeus wrapped his arms around Mabel's shoulders for encouragement.

"I know it's best, but I don't want to see him in pain right now." She stared off into the distance. "The look he gave me when he learned the truth tore my heart in two. He's never looked at me that way before, and I don't know if I can stomach it again."

"I understand, but I don't want to lie to him. He's asked me about Thad, and I've deferred it to you. It's not my place to tell him your truth." She'd said her peace with all the respect she could muster. She didn't want to come off as being out of place or disrespectful, but Mabel needed to know Mike's anxiety regarding Thaddeus.

Mabel looked up over her shoulder to Thaddeus for his approval. She then returned her attention to Danielle and nodded.

"You're right, Danielle. After Christmas it is. I just pray the good Lord will give Mike the heart to understand."

Danielle reached for Mabel's hand and squeezed. "I'll be praying with you. I believe that all of this will turn out well, and maybe Mike will see life through a different lens now—a second chance."

Danielle motioned to pull her hand away, but Mabel held on. "And speaking of second chances, Mike told me you two will start planning your wedding after Christmas."

Mabel bunched her eyebrows in confusion, but one side of her lips curled into a half-smile. Danielle couldn't be sure if Mabel was happy or concerned about the news. As for Danielle, the mere mention of a wedding between her and

Mike again caused perspiration to form at the back of her neck.

Danielle swallowed to moisturize her dry throat and treaded with caution. "About that... That was my way of compromise on the subject for now. He doesn't want to wait, and seeing as though he just had a near-death experience, he wants to live now—and that includes getting married as soon as possible."

Mabel released Danielle's hand and ran a finger along her collarbone, her gaze distant. *"Ummm-hmmm."*

Was she getting ideas, too?

Danielle added, "But as I told Thad, getting married is serious business and is not part of the plan. What happens if his memory suddenly comes back and he realizes he was happy with someone else? Or figured his life was better without me? Or—"

Mabel interjected, "I can assure you there was no one else. If you ask me, he's never gotten over you. If he did suddenly regain his memory, one thing he'd be grateful for is that you're here."

Thaddeus added, "I think I might've just said something similar. No matter what was happening in his life before, in the deep recesses of his heart, he had to have feelings for you, or none of this would be happening. Remember, the first person he asked for was you. If it's his feelings you're concerned about, I think that's the least of our problems."

There was no winning in this conversation. And what was the prize anyway? Was she looking for reassurance? A pep talk? Why were they both so much more certain than she was about all this when she had Mike's best interest at heart, too?

Put your fiancée hat back on. You can do this. Mabel thinks you can, Thad thinks you can, and the check in your pocket says you have to.

Danielle breathed deeply and squared her shoulders. "Since we're all in agreement to share the truth about Thad's identity after Christmas, I'm going to head back inside to sit with Mike for a while."

"We'll be sitting downstairs in the cafeteria if you need us. Again, thanks for everything you're doing for Mike.

I know pretending to be his fiancée is a bit unconventional and you didn't have to, but I thank God you love Mike enough to be what he needs right now." Mabel squeezed her neck before leaving.

Way to go, Mabel.

Danielle held on to the doorknob and watched Mabel and Thaddeus disappear around the corner. She was pretending for Mike's good, but why did it feel so wrong?

She pushed open the door, and Mike's head turned in her direction. His eyes settled on her. The old familiar butterflies fluttered in her belly until it tightened. That's why it felt wrong. It had been difficult to end their relationship before, and she couldn't deal if she had to end it again. Her heart didn't care if this arrangement was purely for his healing, not for them to have a real future together.

He smiled. The imagery she'd never been able to delete from her mind. All she wanted to do was throw herself into his arms.

"I was beginning to think you'd left without saying goodbye."

His voice. Deep yet gentle. The bass that could carry the rhythm to the song of her heart.

Danielle strutted over to his bedside and reclaimed his hand and the seat next to his bed.

"I could never do that."

He lifted her hand to his lips.

His touch sent tingles up her arm. Set her skin afire.

Maybe this was how things were supposed to be between them. Perhaps it wouldn't be such a bad thing if Mike didn't regain his memory. This could be their opportunity for a real second chance.

Her heart was already on board with the idea. And with every moment they spent together, maybe her mind would agree to it, too.

CHAPTER SEVEN

I could never do that.

When had Danielle said that to him before? Simple words, but they felt important, like they were an intricate part to understanding their relationship over the past five years.

Mike had spent the better part of yesterday evening wracking his brain, but nothing came of it. He hated not knowing parts of his past. It'd been like his life was a finished puzzle someone crumbled, and he didn't know how to piece it together again.

Some things were slowly coming back to his remembrance.

For example, his brother-like best friend, Kendrick, died in a car accident almost two years ago. Recalling the memory now made the pain fresh. Kennedy now led the company. That was about it. But the two most important pieces to his life that bothered him the most were his mother and her relationship with this Thaddeus McCall person and his relationship with Danielle. He wasn't certain why, but he got the feeling that they were withholding important information.

He didn't miss how Danielle continued to sidestep his questions about the two of them and about Thaddeus. If nothing else bothered him about not having his memory, his skin crawled, tingled, and whatever else it could do when Thaddeus and his mom were in the room together.

What was he missing?

Mike rested the back of his head in his palm and stared up at the ceiling. He'd been working hard to recover memories since Danielle left yesterday—a futile exercise.

"Asking the ceiling for answers, I see," Kennedy called out to him when she walked through the door.

"Hey there. Danielle is coming to take me home. I'm surprised to see you here."

"I know. Saw her in the parking lot and figured I'd race my way up to chat with you before you gave her your full attention. You know how you are when she's in the room: It's like the rest of us aren't even here."

Mike chuckled. "That's probably a stretch from the truth."

"I'm not far off."

Kennedy sat in the chair next to his bed and gazed into his eyes for several seconds before speaking. "So how are you feeling?"

Mike smirked, but thought for a moment about whether he should share his reservations about his mother and Danielle with Kennedy who had always been like a sister to him with her being his late best friend's twin sister. Plus, he'd known her most of his life.

"All things considered, I'm blessed. Happy to be in the land of the living."

"That's a given, but how are you really feeling?"

"It's hard to explain. A little lost. Out of the loop. It's almost as if everyone has this big secret they're withholding from me."

Kennedy nodded.

"I don't know if it's just me and me not having many memories of the last five years of my life, but it seems bigger than that. It's like I said, hard to put into words."

"I get it. We're hoping that having your family around will help with the recollection. That's why we're all going to stay at McCall Resorts this week to help with your post-op care. You made such an impression on Darius while we worked the project that he offered to have you stay as long as you need."

"Look at that smile on your face. What is he offering you?"

Kennedy gave one of those giggles that reminded him of teenage girls. "I guess that's something else you may not remember. We're a couple now. He's good to me, Mike, so you don't have to worry. You approved before all of this happened."

"Well, it sounds like I may be in the way."

"Don't be silly. You're like a brother to me. I wouldn't have it any other way. Besides, Christmas is only a few days away. You can't spend it in the hospital, and staying home alone isn't an option either. I know how much you love Christmas, so I plan to do everything in my power to make sure this one is good for you."

"Honestly, just spending this time with Danielle is what'll make this Christmas special for me." Danielle walked through the door. His reservations were replaced with adoration. The smile she wore was the only gift he needed, but he added, "Even though she won't marry me for Christmas."

Kennedy turned in her seat to face Danielle and chuckled.

"Don't pay him any mind, Kennedy. He knows that his healing is more important than anything else to me right now."

Danielle strutted to his bedside, leaned in, and kissed his forehead. "Have you received your post-op orders and release yet?"

"No. Still waiting. You look beautiful as always. How are you feeling?"

"Good knowing that you get to come home today."

Kennedy sang, "Only one in the room."

Mike and Kennedy chuckled.

"What did I miss?" Danielle asked.

"Nothing. It's just that Kennedy says I act like no one else is in the room when you're around."

"She's just teasing. Kennedy, have you spoken with Darius? Is everything ready for Mike's arrival at the resort?"

"Yep. We're good to go. Mabel is already there. We'll all have lunch in the main house with the McCall family if you're up to it, Mike."

"It'll be nice to eat lunch with someone other than the TV and the smell of disinfectant. Count me in."

Kennedy stood. "Sounds good. Danielle has everything under control, so I'll see you back at the resort in a little while." Kennedy kissed his cheek. "Bye. Don't give Danielle any trouble."

"Hey, when have I ever been a troublemaker? I'm a good patient."

∞

Trouble?

Danielle's heart thundered in her chest at Kennedy's words. How much had she shared with Mike, if anything at all? This guilt she carried weighed like an anchor on her chest. If she didn't tell Mike about her arrangement with Thad soon, would she crumble under its load?

Danielle gripped the steering wheel tight enough for her knuckles to ache. She stole glances at Mike here and there to gauge whether he knew the truth about the real status of their relationship, but nothing in his features made her think he seemed bothered about anything. He smiled, cracked jokes, and carried on conversation like normal.

"You do know you can at least drive the speed limit, babe."

"Just trying to be careful, that's all."

Mike turned up his palm for her to place her right hand in his. He massaged away the trembles. "Everything is gonna be okay, alright?"

"I know. I guess I'm worrying too much. A lot has changed over the last week. I can't take much more, and I don't think you can either."

"We can handle more than we think we can. I think life is proving that to us right now."

You have no idea.

Danielle turned onto a winding road past oversized purple-and-green signage that read, *Welcome to McCall Resorts—A Retreat for the Mind, Body, and Spirit.*

"Does any of this look familiar to you?" Danielle asked.

After a quarter mile past the signage, they passed the curve in the road where Mike's accident happened. Danielle held her breath and took her eyes off the road for a moment to get a quick look at him.

Mike squinted and took in the scenery. He looked through the driver's side window first and then through the passenger's side. He released a heavy breath. "Vaguely. Feels like I should, but doesn't quite ring a bell. So, SCI built this?"

"Yeah. It's beautiful, isn't it?"

They drove past the eighteen-hole golf course, Wellness House, Mick Chateau's restaurant, and one of the five cottages toward the main house, a multi-family mini-mansion—a replica of the one in Georgia—occupied by Darius McCall and his staff. An excessive amount of living space for one person, but who was she to judge?

"Breathtaking, but I'm not surprised. We've always done great work at SCI. Ken had a keen eye and was good about contractor selection." He sighed.

She knew he must have been thinking about his friend, Kendrick. Before she could jump in, he added, "I never get to experience any project we've worked on to this magnitude. We generally see our clients through post construction, and we're on to the next project. To get a chance to stay in this resort is an honor, really."

"If it's anything like I heard about their Georgia resort, we're both in for a treat."

Danielle navigated the car around the semi-circle driveway and parked. She and Mike climbed out of the car. With her hand tucked in his, they strolled toward the French door entrance. The doors swung open. Mabel and Thad greeted them, presenting themselves as a happy couple. Thad's arm snug around Mabel's waist. Mabel's smile was as wide as the open doors.

Mike squeezed her hand probably harder than he intended. Danielle jerked, but couldn't remove her hand from his grip. Her gaze swooped down to their linked fingers, then back up to his eyes. Furrowed brows and tight eyes met hers.

If they were going to make it through Christmas as a happy family intent on encouraging Mike's healing, Thad and Mabel would have to talk now.

With Every Moment

CHAPTER EIGHT

Mike limped toward the entrance of the antebellum-style mini-mansion. Danielle bore some of his weight while their hands were linked. He refused crutches and a wheelchair. He could walk just fine. He only needed a few extra minutes to get used to the wincing pain. Besides, his primary injury was memory loss, according to the doctor. The physical pain he could endure.

The French-style double doors framed his mother and this Thad person. He didn't like the way Thad's hold on her appeared possessive. Every time he was around, Thad held his mother a little too tight for his taste—his arms wrapped around her shoulders or waist. Wouldn't he remember if his mother started dating? And if so, why would she choose this guy? He couldn't shake the feeling that this dude was hiding something. Every time he'd brought it up to his mom while in the hospital, she dismissed him.

He needed answers.

And answers were exactly what he planned to get.

His mother broke her embrace with Thad and encircled her arms around his waist. Her feather-like touch had to do with the fact he'd recently been in an accident. Yet, it was firm enough to remind him of her love. It was the same hug she'd given him whenever he hurt himself growing up. Injuries from falling off his bike and skinning his knees and elbows, skateboard tumbles, and that time he sprang his arm from landing in an awkward position while jumping on a trampoline. It was one of those hugs that assured him everything would be fine.

Except it wouldn't be fine until this Thad person justified his presence.

"Welcome, son." She breathed deeply before she added, "I'm so thankful that you're here with us."

She released him and stepped aside. "And Danielle, if I haven't said it enough, I'm glad he has you. Thank you for all you're doing to help Mike on his road to recovery."

"I wouldn't have it any other way."

There it was again. When had he heard her say that? And why did it feel important?

"Mike, you remember Thad from the hospital? SCI built this resort for his family. Are you up for taking a small tour to see if it brings about any memories from when you worked on the project, or would you rather rest?"

"Mabel, remember, we shouldn't push," Thad said.

He wasn't up to it, but because this Thad person suggested otherwise, he took his mother up on her offer.

Why was Thad so invested in him?

"Sure. We can look around for a bit. I'm already impressed with what I've seen on the drive through the resort. Is Kennedy here?"

"Yeah. She's in the kitchen with Nina."

Danielle piped in, "Oh, I'll go catch up with her while you spend a few minutes with your mom."

"And I guess I'll give you two some time as well," Thad added. He bent forward and whispered something into her ear before disappearing through the foyer.

Mike squinted and ground his teeth at Thad's retreating back. What was it about this man that made him uneasy?

"Alright then. Come, son." Mabel slipped an arm around his waist. He hobbled alongside her through the foyer.

Before taking a left down the hall, he spotted Danielle across the room in the oversized kitchen engrossed in conversation with Nina and Kennedy. Even fifty feet away, his heart still felt her presence and found a new rhythm at the sight of her. She was the only thing that made sense in all of this.

Down the left hall was a powder room, dining room, and two identical office spaces across from each other. They entered one through a sliding barn door. Though decorated, neither appeared as if they belonged to anyone. Or at least they hadn't been personalized—no photos, no certificates of accomplishment. Instead, they were greeted with cocoa-painted walls, an oversized mahogany desk accompanied by an executive leather seat. In front of it were two visitor chairs. To the right a floor-to-ceiling bookcase. In the same area was an ivory sofa, two accent chairs, and a coffee table. Mike moved to the sofa and sat.

"Mom, I need to ask you something, and I want you to be honest with me."

Mabel sat next to him and covered one of his hands with hers. "What's that?"

"Thad. What's up with him?"

She held his gaze. Her chest rose and fell. A soft whoosh of air escaped her lips.

Why was she buying time?

"What do you mean?"

"I mean, why is he always around? I understand SCI built this resort for his family, but that doesn't explain why he's hugged up on you every time you two are together. Whispering in your ear. Holding your hand. Rubbing your shoulders. Are you dating him? Did I approve of him before the accident? Because I feel like he's hiding something. What gives?"

Mabel diverted her gaze to his hand and rubbed her thumb across his knuckles. She sighed again. Even with their hands in his lap, he still felt her breath on his skin.

"Well, I've known Thaddeus since I was in high school. You remember I grew up in Atlanta, right?"

Mike nodded.

"After high school, we both went to Clark Atlanta where I studied business administration and Thad took up biology. Those were good times."

While the background story was good information, it didn't explain this closeness they seemed to share. If she were anyone else, he would have said, *Spit it out,* but she must've had her reasoning for going back almost forty years.

Her eyes rested on the floor-to-ceiling bookshelf behind him. Why was she measuring her words? He'd never known her to do that with him.

"Mom, whatever you have to say, you can just—"

"Hey. There you are," one of the McCall sons said as he entered the office.

His mother's shoulders relaxed. She turned and welcomed the reprieve. "Darius, good to see you."

He bent and kissed her cheek.

"Good seeing you again, too, Miss Mabel. Mike, man, how's it going?"

Mike knitted his eyebrows together. Though he couldn't quite recall any interactions with the man, as hard as he tried to, he knew the man to be Kennedy's beau, Darius McCall. Mike shook Darius' extended hand.

"As well as I can be. You?"

"Just working on getting things up and running around here. What can I do to make your stay comfortable?" Darius perched on the sofa arm and crossed his arms over his chest.

"Honestly, as long as I have food and Danielle, I'm alright. Good lookin' out though."

"You're like a brother to Kennedy, so that means you're like a brother to me. Besides, you worked your butt off to make sure this resort project finished on time. I can't thank you enough for your expertise and professionalism throughout this project."

"No problem, man. I keep hearing that. Just wish I could remember." Mike offered a light chuckle.

"I get it. No sweat."

"You treatin' Kennedy right?"

"Now you're talking like your old self." Darius chuckled, but Mike found nothing funny about what he'd said. Darius straightened up and cleared his throat. "I am. I love Kennedy, so I'll always do what's in her best interest."

"That's all I ask. She's special, so she deserves the best. Take care of her, or you'll have to deal with me."

"That's one thing we won't have to worry about. Oh, hey, I came looking for you guys because we're about to have lunch. Ready to eat?"

Mabel stood. "I sure am."

Of course she'd jump at the opportunity to leave the room. Mike's head pounded. A headache formed as he worked to piece together everything his mother didn't say.

∞

Danielle locked eyes with Mabel who'd just rushed out of one of the offices, her expression a combination of terror and relief. Her eyes bugged, and her lips puckered as she released a breath loud enough for Danielle to hear. Mike was in the room with Darius.

Danielle blocked Mabel's path. "What's the matter? Is Mike okay?"

102

Mabel nodded before she spoke in a hushed voice. "He's fine, but I don't know if I am. Danielle, I'm not ready to talk with him about Thad again, but he cornered me. I'd started telling him about me and Thad's history before Darius walked in. *Whew.* I need a minute."

"I really do think Mike can handle it if you explain the situation to him. His perspective may be a little different since the accident."

Mabel pressed her trembling palm to her chest and bowed her head. "I know." Her voice cracked. Danielle darted her gaze in every direction. *Oh boy. Don't break down on me now.*

Danielle encircled her arms around Mabel's neck. When she felt Mabel relax, she released her.

"Thanks for that. It's just...I blame myself for his accident. Had he not heard the news the first time, we wouldn't be in this situation, you know?"

"Mabel, you can't believe that."

"I know I shouldn't, but I do. My son can't remember the last five years of his life because of my choices, and for me to have to take him through it again seems to be too much."

Danielle agreed.

"Maybe try telling him alone to give him time to process. Having Thad around for the talk may not be such a good idea since he's already drawing his own conclusions about him, but if you need me, I'll be there or nearby."

Mabel smiled for the first time since she'd come into the hall. Her worry lines in her forehead lessened. "I think that's a good idea."

Danielle didn't subscribe to the idea that Mabel was at fault, but she wholeheartedly believed this information was too much. However, Mike was a grown man who needed the truth.

The truth that would set him free—or make him flee.

CHAPTER NINE

The most important benefit out of pretending to be Mike's fiancée, aside from his healing, was Danielle now had the funds to pay for her mother's medical expenses. An enormous burden had been lifted. Though law school would also be paid for because of her arrangement with Thaddeus McCall, having her mother around for an even longer while took precedence.

All morning long, Danielle hadn't been able to quiet the jitters or her inner voice that cautioned her about the day's Christmas dinner. She couldn't be sure if it was because she'd never attended a huge Christmas gathering with family or if it was fear that something would go wrong with Mike finding out about their relationship in a way she hadn't intended.

As an only child born to parents who were also only children in both their families, her circle was naturally small, so the idea of being part of the McCall family dinner excited her. Made her feel like she'd experience Christmas like she often saw in holiday movies. But more often than not, someone spoiled the joy at one point or another.

She prayed that didn't happen today.

Danielle glanced over at her mother in the passenger seat. The smile tugging at the corners of her lips brought joy to Danielle's heart. Yes, this would be an experience for them both. And to top it off, they'd experience Christmas at a magical resort.

"*Ooh,* this looks fancy, Danielle. How can you afford this?"

"Mom, I told you. We're having Christmas dinner with my fiancé Mike and his family. This is his family's new resort."

Bernadette tapped her chin and repeated Mike's name. "You called off your engagement to him so fast, I almost forgot it happened. Why are you two moving so fast now? Are you pregnant?"

Danielle swerved the car, nearly running off the road. "No, Mom. Why would you say that?"

"This is sudden, that's all. It's your life, and I can't tell you what to do, but marriage is serious business. Are you sure you're ready?"

"I've known him for a long time, so it's not that sudden. And as I told you a few days ago, we still love each other."

"I see." Bernadette reached over and pushed a strand of Danielle's hair behind her ear. "You're my only child, so I want to see you happy. And weren't you dating someone else? Brad? Bobby?"

"Brandon, Mom. We're taking a break while I figure this thing out with Mike."

"Does he know what's going on?"

Guilt settled at the pit of Danielle's stomach. "Yes, he knows."

"*Hmmm..*" Her mom made one of those you-must-be-out-of-your-mind faces, but Danielle had been thankful she didn't push. "I just want what's in your best interest."

"Thanks, Mom. Speaking of best interest, I have the money for you to get the medical treatment you need. We don't have to worry about Medicare covering it. Merry Christmas."

Danielle shrugged. Her smile covered her face hoping to spread that joyous energy to her mother, but her excitement was one-sided.

"Why don't you look happy about the news?"

"Something's going on here, and I want to know right now." Bernadette folded her arms across her chest. Her lips twisted. One eyebrow hiked.

"What do you mean? This is my Christmas present to you."

"So, you're telling me you suddenly came up with ten thousand dollars? I'm not buying it."

To tell the whole truth or not?

Danielle ground her teeth and shot her mother a sideways glance. The less people who knew about the arrangement between her and Thad, the better. However, she had good cause for going through with it: Mike's healing.

Money for her mother's healthcare.

Money for law school.

And to be on the receiving end of Mike's love again.

All worthy causes, except she knew her mother well enough to know that she wouldn't approve. But she was a grown woman who was more than capable of making her own decisions. Yet, her mother's opinion mattered.

She released a slow breath, her chest now deflated.

Danielle slowed her car to a stop and parked outside of the McCall estate. She shifted in her seat to face her mother. *May as well get the truth out now.*

"Mom, as I mentioned before, Mike had an accident. He now has little memory of the last five years of his life. As far as he's concerned, we're engaged. When he came out of surgery, his fiancée—me—is the first person he asked for."

Bernadette gasped, but Danielle continued.

"So, his father and mother thought it was a good idea that I pretend to be his fiancée to help him heal. We're hoping that me being the constant in his life will help his memories return."

"Now Dani, you know—"

"Hold on, Mom. Let me finish while I have the nerve to do so. As part of the arrangement, his father has agreed to handle any financial obligations that I have, which is why I don't need a loan to finish law school and why I have the money to pay for your medical treatment."

"I will not be a part of this, Dani. There's no way that any of this can end well."

Danielle heaved a sigh and rested her forehead in her palm. "I don't know what else to do. I want to help him, Mom. You know I've never really stopped loving Mike. This seems to be what's best right now, and if this is the way to do it, then I want to help."

"So what happens when he finds out you all have been lying?"

"I'm kinda hoping it won't get to that. I'm waiting for the right moment to tell him the truth, but I don't think we need to spring too many truths on him all at once."

Bernadette's scrunched eyebrows and pouty lips reminded Danielle of every time she'd gotten into some kind of trouble as a child and had to confess the truth. Punishment always followed. "What do you mean?"

Saying it aloud reminded her of just how messy the situation had become.

"Well, right before Mike's accident, he found out that Thaddeus McCall is his biological father, and that's one of the things he doesn't remember."

"And this Thaddeus McCall is inside?" She pointed toward the entrance.

"Right. It's his family's resort."

"I know your heart is in the right place, Dani, but I don't want any parts of that blood money. My health will be just fine."

Danielle grabbed her mother's hand and rested her forehead against it. "Mom, I know this is all kinda messy right now, but your health is important to me. Will you please just think about it?"

"What kinda nonsense are you getting me into? You should've told me all of this before you dragged me all the way out here. It's nice and all, but is it worth it?"

"If Mike comes out of this good and well, then it will be. Everything else will work itself out. I have to believe that," Danielle recited, more to herself than a response to

Bernadette's question. "But, Mom, I need you with me today. Can you just enjoy the day with me and not worry about everything else?"

Her mother finally cracked a smile. "You're lucky you're my favorite daughter."

"I'm your only daughter, but I'll take that."

Danielle reached over and hugged her mother's neck. "Alright. Time to hang out with my future in-laws."

Bernadette *tsk*ed and shook her head. She opened the door and turned to Danielle one last time before she stepped out of the car. "Lord, help us all."

Her mom's sentiments confirmed her own feelings. With each step toward the grand entrance, the December winds tossed her long strands about—a simultaneous tossing happening in her belly. She hooked her arms inside her mother's, and her wobbly legs carried her to the double doors that swung open before they could even knock.

Mabel's warm face greeted them.

"Hey, Danielle." Mabel wrapped her arms around Danielle's neck. She released her and turned her attention to Danielle's mother. "Bernadette, it's so good to see you."

Bernadette accepted Mabel's outstretched arms and embraced her. "It's good seeing you again, too. You look good."

"Thanks. So do you. Come on in. I'm happy you could join us. I hope you know how much of a blessing Danielle has been to our family."

Mabel is laying it on too thick.

Bernadette shot Danielle one of those she-must-think-I'm-some-kind-of-fool looks. Her eyebrow hiked, and she parted her lips. But Danielle smiled as sweetly as she could, hoping her mother would get the message. This whole shebang already didn't sit right with her mother, and Mabel wasn't helping the situation.

"Thanks for the invitation."

Danielle's balloon-like chest deflated, releasing a breath she didn't realize she was holding.

Lord, please don't let this evening blow up in my face.

"Come on in, and make yourselves comfortable. Christmas dinner will be ready soon. Until then, we're playing a few family games."

113

Mabel moved to the side to allow them entry. Mike hobbled toward the foyer. Danielle released her mother's arm when she caught sight of him. She wrapped an arm around his waist and glanced down at his full weight resting on one foot.

"Babe, why aren't you resting that leg?"

"Merry Christmas to you, too." Mike's full lips covered hers in a quick peck. Even though it lasted a second, the tingles in her body would last far longer. Would he still kiss her if he knew that all of this was just pretend?

But your love for him isn't.

"Sorry. Merry Christmas. Why aren't you resting that leg?"

"Because I'm an able-bodied man who wanted to be the first face his fiancée saw when she arrived, except my mom is faster than me."

Danielle chuckled. She turned to her mom and wondered if she needed to reintroduce them. "Mike, my mom, Bernadette."

"Even with memory loss, there are some things I can't forget. Like beauty. We know where yours come

114

from." Mike embraced Bernadette. Judging from her smile, his compliment lightened her mood.

"Still charming. Merry Christmas, Mike."

Songs from Kirk Franklin's Christmas album played through the home's speaker system. Mixed aromas of hot chocolate, cinnamon, baked breads, and maple that she'd bet was the glaze for a ham teased her nostrils. Her stomach grumbled in response.

Mabel chuckled. "Just a little while longer. Bernadette, wanna come to the kitchen with me? I'll introduce you to the McCall family, and you and I can chat a little."

"Lead the way."

Mabel turned on her heel. Before she followed, Bernadette leaned and whispered into Danielle's ear, "Let me see what kind of soap opera you've got me involved in."

Danielle bit back a smile. Leave it to her mother to dramatize the situation even more than it already was.

CHAPTER TEN

If Danielle didn't know any better, she'd believe she starred in a holiday fairytale romance airing on Netflix.

The atmosphere was perfect.

Almost too perfect.

And the mere fact caused a queasiness in the pit of her belly she couldn't shake. No water, Pepto Bismol, sparkling cider, ginger ale, or nibbling on crackers could cure it. The only cure would be walking away with everyone's heart and feelings intact. And by everyone, that meant Mike.

The McCall sons, Andrew and Darius, along with Kennedy and Nina gathered around the coffee table with her and Mike playing board games. Danielle won a game of Scrabble. As a team, she and Mike won their game of

Christmas charades. She'd forgotten how well they worked together. Even after five years of being apart, they were still connected as if no time had elapsed. The biggest win was Mike snuggled next to her, whispering *I love you* and how happy he was to have her by his side.

She caught Nina glancing in her direction every now and then throwing her sly smiles and winks. While she appreciated the encouragement, she couldn't help but wonder how long it would last. Would Mike find out today that their engagement was a farce? Would it ruin Christmases to come for him? Or would he see it as honorable on her part? Would it make him love her more?

"Alright, last game before dinner," Kennedy announced. Her dark, curly hair shone just as bright as her smile. She reached under the farmhouse storage coffee table, opened a drawer, and removed a set of Uno cards. "There's a prize for the winner, so put your game faces on."

"I've been trying to help her practice, y'all, but it didn't work. I beat her every single time," Darius chimed in.

The group chuckled.

"Don't believe the hype. I win against him in every game we play," Kennedy said.

"I might lose in Uno, but I won't lose the cookie challenge," Nina added.

Danielle scrunched her eyebrows in confusion. "What's that?"

"No one told you?" Nina glanced around the coffee table. "We're having a cookie bake-off after dinner. The kitchen is already fully stocked, so no excuses. Everyone bakes their best batch of cookies. Winner gets bragging rights for the entire year."

"I'm not really a baker, so I'll let you handle that, babe. I'll be the judge," Andrew said.

Darius shook his head. "Nah. He just doesn't like to lose."

Danielle diverted her attention to Andrew's brother, Darius. "So, Darius, I take it you can bake."

"I can do a little something. Mike, are you in?"

"Yep. I won't turn down the opportunity for bragging rights, but are y'all sure you wanna risk it—bragging rights going to an outsider, someone who isn't part of your family? May as well decide now to have a second-place winner."

An awkward chuckle and darting eyes followed. Hopefully, Mike didn't pick up on the discomfort that seemed to pass between the group because of what he didn't know about his relationship to them, but Danielle did. That was not the path they needed to walk. She interjected. "First things first, let me claim my crown in Uno."

∞

Though Mike wasn't sure what his last few Christmases were like, he ranked this Christmas as one of his best as an adult. Like Danielle, he grew up as an only child, but at least he had Kendrick and Kennedy. They practically grew up together as siblings. And to see the light in Kennedy's eyes today made his heart swell like that of a proud big brother. Surely, Darius McCall had something to do with the twinkling in her eyes.

And even though he wasn't one of them, the McCall family treated him like one of their own. He felt like a relative based on the kindness they'd shown him. From the free stay at the resort to every one of them checking in on him at one point or another, if he didn't know any better, he'd say they considered him to be a McCall. Even this Thad person appeared to be a good guy and not what he'd expected. He checked in on him and insisted he got everything he needed. Mike sensed sincerity coming from him. Perhaps he'd judged him too quickly. But what was he supposed to do, given that every time he saw him, Tad held his mother's hand or wrapped his arm around her waist or shoulder? Thankfully, there had been little of that today.

If no one else was around, his day would have been just as swell with Danielle around. The way she leaned into his side whenever he whispered, "I love you," stirred the depths of his soul, set his skin on fire through the layers of clothing between them. The way she smiled at him, almost shyly, like their relationship was new. And her presence alone made it feel like Christmas because she was a gift to him, in and of herself.

Maybe it was a good thing he didn't remember what their relationship was like before the accident. This freshness, this newness he felt, he wanted it to stay.

With Every Moment

Rose McCall, mother of the brothers, appeared in the doorway dressed in a festive holiday sweater and Santa felt hat. She shook a little bell. "Dinner is ready, my loves. You all can head to the dining room and find your place setting."

"Uno out," Danielle shouted and tossed her last card onto the discard pile. "What is that? Three times in a row?"

"Yeah, there's some cheating going on," Andrew said.

Danielle taunted. "The tune of a loser."

Their group burst into laughter, and one by one, stood.

"Well, I want another rematch," Darius said.

Something told him that the brothers, Andrew and Darius, didn't take losing well.

Mike was the last to stand, declining help from the group. He winced when he put pressure on his sore leg. Danielle linked her fingers in his and walked alongside him down the double wide hall to the dining room. Freshly baked cornbread, candied yams, and mustard greens overpowered the aromas of everything that would be served. Or maybe it was his own personal preferences that pinpointed his favorite holiday foods. Even with the loss of important memories, his favorite foods were something he didn't think he could ever forget.

"Who did the cooking?" Danielle asked.

"Mrs. Rose and my mom."

"Your mom's cooking is good. I'm so ready for Christmas dinner. I skipped breakfast so that I could have room to eat everything on the spread."

"You know that doesn't work, right? You'll be full even faster than you normally would since you didn't eat breakfast."

"Yeah, I know, but I'm hoping for a different turnout today." Danielle patted her belly.

"Well, I'm more than happy to share my food with you should you need more."

"I'll remember that when I come for your chocolate cake."

Mike threw his head back and chuckled. One day Danielle would realize she could have anything she wanted from him.

With Every Moment

The grand dining table had twelve place settings, though they didn't have a twelfth person. Jeff McCall, the family's patriarch, sat at the head of the table with his wife, Rose, to his right and his brother Thad to his left. Andrew, Nina, Darius, and Kennedy filled the seats next to Rose. Mabel, Mike, Danielle, and her mother, Bernadette, filled the seats next to Thaddeus.

Jeffrey's voice boomed. "Before we bless the food on our table, let me be the first to welcome Kennedy, Mabel, Mike, Danielle, and Bernadette. Your presence adds even more joy to this special occasion. As we celebrate Jesus' birth, we are also thankful that you've chosen to share in this time with us. Shall we pray?"

The group bowed their heads as Jeffrey led them in prayer. "Father God, thank You for a fresh opportunity to celebrate Jesus' birth. Thank You for the new friends—well, family—that you brought into our lives. Help us keep You in the center of this season. Bless our table once again. Bless the cooks. Allow this food to be nourishing to our bodies and accepted with grateful hearts. In Jesus' name, everyone say…"

"Amen."

For the next several minutes, the only sounds were the clinking of silverware against serving dishes and murmurs of "please pass" this and that. Mike was nearly satiated from looking at the entrées. Everything appeared to be cooked to perfection: dinner rolls, cornbread, Cornish hens, mustard greens, maple-glazed ham, green bean casserole, candied yams baked with marshmallows, oven baked macaroni and cheese, cornbread dressing, and a few other dishes he couldn't identify but planned to eat.

After his first bite, Mike said, "Mom and Mrs. Rose, everything looks so good. I appreciate your hard work."

Mabel leaned over and nudged his shoulder. "You know it's my pleasure, son. I also had to make sure I had all of your favorites. It's a blessing that you're sitting at this table with us. That's my Christmas gift."

Thad piped in. "We're all thankful for your recovery, Mike."

The group added similar sentiments. Though he appreciated it, he didn't like to be the center of attention, so he changed the subject.

"Mrs. Rose, what's your favorite dish to cook?"

"Oh, honey, none of that Mrs. Rose stuff. That's too formal. You're practically family. Please call me Aunt Rose."

Mike assumed she said that because of his relationship with Kennedy since she and Darius were pretty cozy these days. Or did it have something to do with his mother and Thad? He'd hang on the former.

"Alright, Aunt Rose. Let's hear it."

"I actually prefer experimenting with baking. I don't mind getting a little dirty with flour. My specialty is apple pie, which you'll get to try later, but I have the golden touch when it comes to just about anything I bake."

"So, does that mean you're going to win this cookie bake-off I just heard about?"

"I'm not even sure if it'll be fair for me to participate."

Nina couldn't swallow her food fast enough to jump into the conversation. "So Momma Rose, is that a challenge—or better yet, can we do this in teams? I've been losing all day. I need a win."

The group erupted into laughter.

"Babe, does that mean you're trying to team up with my mom instead of me?" Andrew pouted toward Nina in a way Mike would rather not have seen.

Andrew Jr. cried on cue. Nina leaped from her seat and removed him from the bassinet to coddle him.

Andrew nodded toward the baby. "See, even Junior feels his dad's pain."

"How about we team up in three groups, pull numbers to make it fair and keep feelings from getting hurt," Rose announced.

The group agreed. They finished up dinner, with some of them receiving second helpings, and loaded the dishwasher. Leftovers were covered and stored in the refrigerator.

Rose numbered sheets of paper, dropped them in a jar, and shook. The group stood around the chef's island and passed the jar. After everyone pulled numbers, they were divided into three teams: Team 1 was Andrew, Darius, Jeffrey, and Kennedy. Team 2 was Mike, Thad, Mabel, and Bernadette. Team 3 was Nina, Danielle, and Rose.

"I'm the oddball on this mother, father, and son team. Can I join team 3?" Bernadette asked.

Mike bugged his eyes so wide, he felt a twinge of pain on his lids. "What did you say?"

Everyone's heads whipped in Bernadette's direction. She bit her lip as if suddenly remembering she wasn't supposed to mention that information. Mike glanced around the room. Everyone wore the same *I'm sorry* expression.

So was that the reason Thad was hanging around? Somehow Thad was supposed to be his father? Mike shook his head. No, his father was Victor Stewart. He gripped the kitchen island. His eyes darted to his mother. Tears sprang to her eyes. His belly sank, and not from the food he'd eaten. Did he know this before the accident?

Mike shook his head again. His fingers trembled. His head hurt and was now heavy to the point he thought it would burst. Danielle slid closer and rubbed his back. In ordinary circumstances, her touch would have made things better.

But it didn't.

One glance in her direction told him she knew about Thad, too. Didn't he ask her about Thad while he was in the hospital? And just how long had everyone known this? And why did they think him incapable of handling the truth?

CHAPTER ELEVEN

"My Lord. Me and my big mouth. I'm so sorry." Bernadette pressed her fist to her mouth. Her eyes appeared larger, yet softer. She was genuinely sorry.

"Ms. Bernadette, none of this is your fault," Mike said. He didn't look at Bernadette. His eyes were glued to his mother's.

Thad being his father would explain why she looked scared to death every time he asked her about Thad's business concerning him. Did she have an affair while married to Victor? Was he adopted? None of this was making any sense.

"If you all don't mind, will you please give me and my mom a minute?"

Without a word, the group dispersed. Because they were so quiet, it reminded him of movie scenes when family and friends would leave the room, but remain silent so they could be nosey.

Thad stayed behind. "I think this is a conversation the three of us need to have."

"If you don't mind, I need to talk to my mom alone first."

Mabel interjected. "He's right, Mike. This is a conversation that involves the three of us."

His chest tightened and ached. Danielle cuffed his arm, and the tension eased. "Babe, do you want me to stay with you?"

"I'm alright. I need a moment with my mom. Give me a minute." He kissed her cheek.

Danielle rubbed her hand along his back before she stepped away. This time, her touch was more comforting than the last. It was as if her touch had words all on its own, reminding him that everything would work out fine.

The room cleared.

With Every Moment

Only Mike, Mabel, and Thad were left. The thickness and heaviness of the silence could not be measured. If he didn't know any better, he'd believe he was wedged between some type of machine that had the sole purpose of squeezing the breath out of him. His breathing became heavier with him forcing air in and out.

Mabel and Thad's eyes locked in on him, giving him time to process the news, which he didn't like because those moments left room for him to conjure up his own story about what happened.

Finally, he said, "Did I know Thad was my biological father before the accident?"

"Yes."

Mike's face grew warm. Her short answer said more than what she didn't say. What was she trying to hide from him? Though Thad stood next to her, Mike's eyes never left hers.

"For how long? And please, Mom, don't make me beg for answers. This is my life—my identity—we're talking about here. I want to hear everything right now."

Mabel rubbed along her arms like she was cold, but that couldn't be the case because he wore a short-sleeved shirt, and his skin was on fire. Mabel pulled a barstool from beneath the chef's island and sat.

"Thad and I went to high school and some of college together at Clark Atlanta. We dated the entire time. Thad was so good to me, but then I got pregnant during the summer before our senior year. I left Atlanta and moved to Houston with my grandmother. I didn't tell Thad about you at the time because I was scared and he would soon be on his way to medical school. I didn't want to interfere with that, nor did I want him to do anything to jeopardize his future. I knew he would become a great doctor."

She stopped and glanced in Thad's direction. His eyes were now misty.

"I know it wasn't right, but in my twenty-year-old mind, it made sense. I'd always planned to tell him about you, but time went on, and then I met Victor when you were three years old. You took to him so easily. It was like we were meant to be a family. We married within nine months, and he adopted you as his own. By that time, Thad was in medical school. I didn't think it wise to rock the boat, especially when things were going so well."

Mike's gaze held hers, though he couldn't see her. He gulped a cup of water to moisten his dry throat and with hopes to cool his rising temperature and pulse. His mother had lied to him his entire life. What else was she keeping from him?

Thad handed a napkin to Mabel. She wiped her eyes, took a deep breath, and continued.

There's more.

Her words were choppy, but she continued. "I hadn't spoken to Thad since I left Atlanta pregnant with you. He walked into the office building for the McCall Resorts grand opening a couple of weeks ago. He took one look at you and did the math. That's when you learned he is your biological father and when Thad found out he had a son—right before the accident."

Mabel sobbed, blew her nose, and sobbed some more. Thad rubbed her back and kissed the top of her head.

"So, the accident was my fault, son. Your memory would be just fine and we wouldn't be having this conversation if I didn't keep you two apart all these years. I'm sorry. I'm so sorry. I did what I thought was best back then."

Mabel cried more.

As much as he didn't agree with her choices, he couldn't allow her to shoulder the blame for his accident. Nor could he watch her bawl her eyes out. He'd never witnessed such a scene from her. Not even when they lost Victor.

Mike hobbled around the chef's island and took the seat next to her. He pulled her into his arms and squeezed until her crying subsided. But then his own tears sprang to his eyes.

"Mom, you can't blame yourself for the accident. You couldn't predict what would happen, and you didn't control the actions of the truck driver. I don't blame you, so please don't do this to yourself."

Where were they supposed to go from here?

Mike swallowed the knot in his throat, which seemed more like shards of glass. He attempted to clear his throat three times before speaking. He looked at Thad with fresh eyes. At least now it made sense why he was always around.

"And you? What do you think of all this?"

"I was angry at Mabel when I found out. I'd been robbed of the one thing I've never had—a child of my own. Now, look at you. You're a grown man with your own life. You don't need a father anymore. I missed out on so much: time I can never get back, time with you, time with your mother. I've always loved her. Still do."

Mike looked from one to the other.

"I know you need some time to process this, Mike, but if you are willing, I'd like to get to know you."

Thad was right: He needed time.

How much? He didn't know.

This wasn't quite the Christmas gift he expected, but he refused to allow the news to ruin one of his favorite holidays. The better question was what else didn't he know that everyone else had decided he was too fragile to handle?

As much as he desired answers, he wouldn't push for more than he could bear today. Those answers had to wait.

∞

All eyes burned a hole through Bernadette's skull while their ears tuned in to the conversation between Mike, Thad, and Mabel happening in the next room. When Danielle could no longer take their judging eyes, she buried her face in her hands.

I'm sorry you had to find out this way.

Jeffrey's voice boomed, cutting through Danielle's thoughts. "The good news is that man knows the truth now. He can take it all in, figure out how to deal with it, and move on with his life."

Rose moved to Jeff's side and perched on the chair arm he occupied. "You know, Jeff is right. Why are we sitting around here acting like Bernadette did something wrong when obviously Mike needed to know the truth? It isn't for us to judge when he hears it. Mike is an adult. He can work through this."

Words of agreement echoed throughout the parlor. Rose was right, but that didn't make Danielle feel any better. How was Mike taking the news? And how would that affect what he thought of her when he found out she was pretending to be his fiancée? And not only was she

136

pretending, but Thad was paying her to do so. In her mind, the money was a bonus, and though she needed it, she would've helped Mike if Thad didn't pay her. But would Mike see it that way?

"And Danielle," Nina added as she paced the floor rocking Andrew Jr., "We all know how much you love Mike, but you can't fix this for him either. Just love him and be there for him."

Danielle nodded and wiped a tear that escaped. So easy for Nina to say when she was living her happily ever after with her first love, in a mansion, on a resort, with their first child.

"Right. Mike is family. Everyone in this room is family. So, Bernadette, you're not to blame for any of this. I hope you understand that," Rose said.

In the short time Danielle had known her, she'd already taken a liking to the woman.

Bernadette relaxed against the back of the sofa and spread her arm behind Danielle. She had one of those looks on her face as if to say, *I know it isn't my fault.* And Danielle prayed she didn't verbalize it.

"Thanks, Rose. But I'm curious: How long were y'all planning to keep Mike from knowing that man is his daddy?"

A long bout of silence passed, each person in the room looking from one to the other.

Jeffrey slid forward in his seat and clasped his hands. "Well, Bernadette, this is a delicate situation considering Mike had just found out about Thad prior to his accident. His parents thought it best to share the news with him when they felt he could receive it. As for us," he said, fanning his hand, "it wasn't our place to tell him."

"*Ummm-hmmm.*" Bernadette looked to Danielle and whispered, "Soap opera."

Mike appeared in the doorway. His presence commanded silence. "We're ready for the cookie challenge, but we're gonna have to shuffle around the teams."

One side of his lip turned upward. His eyes found hers, and everything she'd eaten earlier seemed to slosh around. She couldn't read him. Did Thad and Mabel tell Mike about their arrangement with her? Was he upset? Was he waiting her out to see if she'd tell him the truth? No, Mike wouldn't do that. If he knew something, he would ask to talk about it.

She glanced down at her hands in her lap. She'd been so nervous that she'd dug her nails into the back of her hand. She couldn't go on like this—wondering if Mike would find out and think of her as being selfish. Or that she only stayed to help because of the money. After today, she'd tell him the truth. Whether he wanted her to go or stay, she'd oblige his wishes.

But what she couldn't do was keep pretending.

CHAPTER TWELVE

By far, that had to be the most interesting Christmas Day he'd experienced—as far as he could remember.

When Danielle mentioned the Christmas festival downtown and that they'd get to do the hayride, he jumped at the opportunity. That's one of the last memories he had of the two of them together—when he proposed. He figured she wanted to help get his problems off his mind, an escape he desperately needed after receiving the news about Thad.

He stole glances at her behind the steering wheel. She seemed more rigid this evening. Sure, the temperature had dropped to the upper fifties, which warranted a light coat, but the way she gripped the steering wheel and engaged him in conversation was robotic. He prayed she didn't have a secret, too. He couldn't take another one of those so soon.

"Babe, are you alright? Seems like something may be bothering you."

Danielle turned her attention from the road for a second and flashed an I-love-you smile. "I'm alright. Worried about you a little. Are you sure you're okay?"

"Talking about the situation with Thad?"

"Yes. I didn't want to bring it up if you weren't ready to talk about it. Just want to make sure you're okay. I know that's a lot to take in—learning the man you thought was your biological father had adopted you."

Mike released a half-hearted chuckle. "I gotta tell you it's not what I was expecting, but I knew something was up with him. But with the way my life is going and the fact that I almost lost it, I don't want to hold on to the past." Mike paused and stared out the window at the twinkling holiday lights strung on top of houses and office buildings. "You know, it's hard to believe my mom could keep something like this away from me, but since she's always worked to provide a good life for me, I know her intentions were good."

At least that's the truth he wanted to believe—what he held on to so that he wouldn't succumb to anger.

For a while, Danielle didn't speak. She nodded and gave him time to process. That was one thing he adored about her. It was as if they could feel each other and knew what the other needed. And he needed a quiet moment.

After the moment passed, she asked, "So what's going to happen with you and Thad? Are you going to get to know him?"

"Eventually, I hope we can get to that point. Like I told him, I don't know when it will happen, but I'm open to it."

Danielle removed one hand from the steering wheel and covered his hands. Warmth ravaged his skin. It amazed him how the smallest touch from her could set his world back on its rightful axis. What is the real reason they hadn't married before now? That excuse she gave at the hospital about focusing on her career and law school didn't feel like the whole story.

He'd make it a point to find out the truth tonight, especially since they were going back to the place where it all began.

∞

With Every Moment

Danielle and Mike strolled to the passenger pick-up area hand-in-hand. They joined the line waiting to climb aboard the hay-filled trailers. With today being the final day of the Christmas hayride, Danielle expected to see more of a crowd. Perhaps the rest of the town had enjoyed this activity sooner. If she and Mike were a real couple and his accident hadn't happened, they would have done it weeks ago. But given the situation he was in, she hoped the Christmas hayride would cheer him up.

He didn't mind sitting on fresh stacks of hay admiring millions of lights, sipping hot chocolate, and listening to Christmas music. She loved all those things, too, minus the itchy, sticky hay. Something about riding on hay just didn't seem normal to her, but she'd muddle through it because it brought a smile to his face. Besides, this hayride was one of the happiest memories she shared with him over five years ago.

What was she hoping to accomplish here?

She hoped it would spark some sort of memory to help her out when she got to the part where she dared tell him the whole truth about the current status of their relationship.

She hoped he would be in a good mood to receive it.

Understand her heart and the position she was in.

Understand the why.

And understand that her intentions were pure—always believing that sticking around would aid in his recovery.

While waiting to climb atop the trailer, they chatted with the couple ahead of them, dressed in their Christmas sweaters and beaded bell necklaces. The hayride had been a tradition of theirs since they married seven years ago. A sadness hung over Danielle. Though it wasn't her favorite thing to do, the hayride could've just as easily been a yearly tradition of hers and Mike's had she not broken their short-lived engagement. Her solemnity must have shown on her face because Mike tugged at her hand. She plastered on a smile and jumped back into the conversation.

A vendor whom she hadn't noticed before now called to the crowd, announcing the sale of hot chocolate. Mike's eyes lit up, and she got the message. He mainly drank it to keep warm.

"You rest that leg, and I'll run over and grab us a cup."

Danielle strolled over to the makeshift stand, which was nothing more than a truck's tailgate unfolded and a cardboard sign spray-painted in red. The older white-bearded gentleman wore a Santa suit with the matching red felt hat.

"Merry Christmas, young lady. I hope you receive everything on your wish list this year."

Danielle handed him the money.

"Thank you. Merry Christmas. This has been one Christmas I'll never forget."

He winked and handed her two cups of hot chocolate covered with lids.

"I take it that's a good thing. God bless you, and remember that Jesus is the reason for the season."

"Amen."

Danielle accepted the cups and walked back over to where Mike stood.

"Thanks, babe." He kissed her lips. "It's about time to climb on. Need me to hold your cup?"

"Sure. Thanks."

Danielle handed Mike both cups and climbed aboard, hay crunching beneath her feet. Thankfully, she'd taken her allergy medicine that morning so she wouldn't have a sneeze attack. The tune of "Silent Night" played through the speakers, something she hadn't noticed before. She'd been too caught up in her own bungled thoughts. When she found herself comfortable, she leaned over and took both cups from Mike so that he could join her. He was the last person to come aboard. He winced and groaned a little as he climbed up and settled in the space next to her.

The driver ensured they were all comfortable on the raised hay seating before climbing behind the wheel of the truck. A slight jolt forward, and they were on their way. The sun set. The sparkling lights became more visible and beautiful. She snuggled against Mike's rigid chest and sipped her hot chocolate. The last time they'd done this, she remembered thinking that she could spend every Christmas season with him, just like that.

Except she didn't.

And she couldn't.

Not with the depression and pain of her parents' health weighing her down.

In hindsight, she probably should have drawn closer to him and the comfort he wanted to give her, but she couldn't see past her pain, and she didn't want to bring him down with her. Yes, her choice made sense to her back then, but now she wished she'd made a different choice. Then she wouldn't have to pretend to live the life she desired to live with him. She could be his. And he could be hers. Forever.

But that wasn't her truth.

She could only pray that Mike would understand when she shared it with him.

They'd been on the hayride tour about an hour, and it was ending. Her pulse escalated as the trailer came to a stop. What thoughts had been going through Mike's mind? Did the ride bring about any memories for him?

When the ride ended, Mike was the first to descend. He attempted to stretch but stopped short because of his pain.

"Remind me not to sit for that long again. I think that ride may have done me more harm than good. Everything is stiff. I think my lower back hurts the most." He massaged the area then reached to take her hand in his so that she could climb down.

"Oh. Sorry about that. I didn't think about your injuries when I suggested we take the ride."

"I know your heart was in the right place."

They strolled to a nearby bench and sat.

"You know the one thing I can't wrap my head around, Dani?"

"What's that?" Now her fingers trembled, matching the uptick in her pulse. He used her name instead of terms like *babe* or *sweetheart*.

"We've been engaged for five years. Why haven't we gotten married? I know waiting this long couldn't have been my idea because I can't imagine my life without you. Tell me. How did this happen?"

Danielle swallowed the hot chocolate that seemed to have made its way out of her stomach and back up to her throat. It'd been settled there about thirty minutes. Ugh.

148

Before now, she'd convinced herself that she was prepared to have this conversation with Mike, but the earnest look in his eyes, the purity, the love, was her undoing. She looked toward heaven and whispered a silent prayer. However, Mike dealt with the revelation, she would accept.

Danielle slid closer until their bodies touched and squeezed Mike's hands in her own. She swallowed one last time. She parted her lips, but the words wouldn't come. Something inside of her cautioned her to wait another day. That telling him now wouldn't end well. But he'd asked, and she had to give him the truth.

Dear God, you know my heart. Let Mike see it, too.

"We didn't get married because we broke up." She gauged his reaction. His grip loosened, but he didn't let go. Danielle took that as a sign to continue.

"Five years ago when you proposed, my dad had recently died, and I'd just found out about my mom's sickness. I was depressed, angry, and just in a funky mood altogether. I didn't think I was in the best place emotionally to intertwine my life with yours long term. About two weeks into our engagement, we stopped seeing each other to give me the time I needed. It was supposed to be temporary, but eventually I gave the ring back to you. I was immature and just not ready for the commitment,"

"I don't understand. Then, how are you here now?" Mike scrunched his eyebrows, the lines in his forehead deeper than she'd ever seen.

"I saw you right before your accident. Nina invited me to the ribbon cutting ceremony at the McCall Resort. That was the first time we'd seen each other in five years. We agreed to go for coffee after the ceremony, but after you found out about Thad, you left, and that's when you had the accident. When you woke up from surgery, I was the first person you asked for—your fiancée."

Mike's eyes grew large, but Danielle continued while she still had the courage to do so.

"I didn't have the nerve to correct you, especially after everything you'd been through. And Thad and Mabel thought it was a good idea for me to go along with it hoping it would help your recovery, so I did. Because I never stopped loving you, and I wanted to do my part to help."

Tell him about the money.

"I don't know what to say."

Danielle bit her lower lip. How could she tell him about the money in a way that he'd understand her intentions were pure—that the money didn't matter?

"There's something else you should know." Every muscle in her body contracted. A tingle made its way down her spine. Her body shivered even though her coat kept her warm. "Thad agreed to pay my tuition and my mother's medical expenses if I agreed to help. He didn't want me to focus on my own problems, but solely on you."

Mike wriggled his hands free of hers and put space between them on the bench. His eyes watered. His mouth moved, but no words came.

Please say something.

"So was I a charity case to you? Is the money the only reason you agreed to stay?"

Danielle slid closer and gripped his arm. "No. Of course not. Mike, you know I love you."

Mike peeled her fingers from his bicep.

"Do I? You made a fool of me. I've been asking you about a wedding for goodness' sake. Were you planning to go through with the marriage, too?" Mike ran all ten fingers through his short waves.

"I–I–"

"When exactly were you planning to tell me the truth, Dani?"

"Babe, I–"

"Stop it. Don't call me that. You don't have to pretend anymore."

"It's not like that. Will you just listen?"

Mike wouldn't even look at her. He now sat hunched over with his hands fisted between his knees. "Where's the money?"

She hadn't spent the money she planned to use for her mother's medical expenses. Her mother didn't agree with the arrangement she had with Thad, but sharing that information with Mike would likely solidify his feelings. It wasn't right. Almost like blood money. But couldn't he understand she thought her mother needed it, that it was necessary for her health?

Danielle remained silent.

"That's what I thought. You can leave."

"But, babe, I mean Mike—"

"Leave. I'm not your charity case, and I don't want you in my life if you aren't here for the right reasons. I can find my way back home. Bye, Dani."

Danielle leaned in to kiss Mike good-bye. When she got close, he moved away. She would have bet money that her heart physically broke into pieces because that space in her chest burned and sizzled.

And not in a good way.

She stood and took a deep, steadying breath. She didn't turn around to look at him, but said, "Money or not, I stayed because I love you. I missed you. And I hoped that somewhere in all of this, we would find us again and have the life we always dreamed we'd have."

Danielle rushed back to her vehicle, hoping to make it before the tears fell. She made it to her car and climbed behind the wheel in the nick of time. She couldn't start the ignition because tears flooded her eyes and cheeks the second she locked the doors.

She released one of those ugly cries, one where she had to blow her nose several times.

One where she nearly choked on air.

One that she had a hard time reeling in.

She couldn't stop the tears from flowing.

What made her think this would work out in her favor? That Mike would see her heart and know that ultimately she made the choice to be his fiancée because that's what she wanted? Him.

Always him.

CHAPTER THIRTEEN

Paying Danielle to be his fiancée?

Where did they do things like that other than books and television? And to think his mother was in on such an agreement made his skin feel like an army of ants was crawling on him.

Disgusted.

Betrayed.

How did any of them think this was supposed to end?

Mike stood when Kennedy arrived on site. He'd called her when Danielle left. She was about the only person he could depend on right now. If he hadn't been able to reach her, his next bet would have been an Uber or Lyft.

Kennedy hopped out of the car and shuffled to his side. She stretched her neck to the left and right, then over his shoulder. "Where's Danielle?"

"I sent her home."

"Why? What happened?"

"Let's just go, Kennedy. I don't want to talk about it right now."

Her shoulders slumped, and her doe-like eyes searched his. Without saying a word, she could sense his pain. They'd been friends long enough for her to know something was wrong—and he was glad about it—because he didn't want to have the Danielle conversation right now. She turned on her heel, and he caught sight of a sparkle coming from her left ring finger.

He reached for her hand. "Whoa. What is this?"

She squealed. He could've sworn he saw all her teeth. "Darius proposed."

"Congratulations. I'm happy for you."

"Thanks, Mike. Things have been going so well between us, but I didn't think it would happen so soon. I just wish—" Her words trailed off, and he knew she was about to mention her late twin brother, Kendrick. Instead, she started toward the car. "Let's get you back to the estate."

"No." His voice was firm enough to halt her tracks. "Take me home."

Kennedy nodded and climbed behind the wheel. When Mike secured himself in the passenger seat, she started the engine and navigated the car back to the main road. A few silent minutes into the ride, she asked, "You sure you want to go home and be alone right now? I mean, it's still the holiday season, and it's your favorite time of the year."

Going back to McCall Resorts would remind him of the time he'd spent with Danielle yesterday, and seeing Thad and his mother would remind him of their part in this game they played with his life.

"It's probably for the best, Kennedy. I don't think I can look at my mom or even stomach Thad right now."

She took her eyes off the road for a second and glanced in his direction.

"Tell me what happened."

Though he hated to rehash the details because he'd done that twice since Danielle left, he did a third time to Kennedy. Perhaps he'd gain clarity if he spoke it aloud to someone other than himself. Kennedy nodded as she listened, but she didn't murmur a word. When he finished retelling the story, she still didn't speak. How much of this did she know?

"Let me guess: None of this is news to you."

"Some of it. I know you've always loved Danielle, and I believe that somewhere inside you hoped the two of you would find your way back to each other again. When you woke up from surgery asking for her, I figured those were your suppressed feelings manifesting. And like your mom and Thad, I thought it was a good idea to let it play out—that maybe being with Danielle would somehow help you get your memories back. But I didn't know that he paid her."

"That's what bothers me the most." Mike propped his elbow against the door handle and rubbed his chin stubble. His heart rate escalated at the speed of a jackhammer at the thought of Danielle accepting money to be with him. "I can't believe she would take money to be with me. I've always been good to her, to my recollection. Always loved her with everything in me. Always gave her the best of me. And she could only do that if money was on the line."

"But," Kennedy's voice was soft and hesitant, "how do you know she did it solely for the money?"

"How do I not?" His voice rose an octave. "She was pretending to be my fiancée. Was she going to marry me, too? How long would this have gone on? Would he have had to pay extra for her to bear my children?"

Kennedy shot him an incredulous look. Her eyebrows shot up so far that he thought they'd reach her hairline. Yeah, that sounded ludicrous, even to him, but how could he be certain of her feelings at all?

"Mike, do you really believe that? Can you truthfully say that you believe Danielle doesn't love you?"

He could only pray it wasn't pretend.

The way she felt in his arms wasn't pretend.

The way his heart wrote a new rhythm every time she came around wasn't pretend.

The way her lips felt against his wasn't pretend.

And his love for her was as real as there were thirty-one days in December.

She had to feel the same way, too. No amount of money could make her fake it, could it?

"I don't know if I can trust my feelings. All I can see are the facts before me, and they don't look good."

"You want my opinion?"

He really didn't. His hurt wanted to hold on to what he believed was real—they all betrayed him—but he fanned his hand and gave her permission to share her thoughts.

"I think," she said, jamming a finger to her chest, "that Thad was desperate. He'd just found out that you were his son, and he wanted to do anything possible to ensure he'd get to have a relationship with you. Danielle was desperate to help in any way she could because she loves you. I honestly believe that she would've made the same choice even if Thad didn't offer her any money. And of course, your mom would've done anything to ensure your recovery. So they were all desperate and willing to do crazy things to help you. They did none of this to hurt you. You have to believe that."

He wanted to believe it.

But right now, he couldn't see past the hurt and the audacity of his family to toy with his life.

Kennedy pulled up to his house and parked in the driveway. He'd hoped going home would help put away thoughts of Danielle for a while, but one look at the house flooded his thoughts with memories of her. Danielle had been the one who accompanied him on his house search. He decided on the brick, one-story, three-bedroom home because she liked it. As for him, two-story or one-story, the number of bedrooms and subdivision didn't matter as much to him, but her opinion did. On the day he closed, he'd been certain that one day she'd move in with him as his wife, but that never happened.

He couldn't bring himself to go inside. How had he managed to not think about her in five years—or had that been the case?

"On second thought, take me back to the resort."

∞

After that scene with Mike at the hayride Danielle drove to the senior living community and picked up her mom to stay the night at her house. Even though she'd lived alone since college, she didn't want to spend the night by herself. Her nightmare had manifested, just as she believed it would when Thad first presented the idea of the fake fiancée arrangement. Even though she loved Mike, look at where it got her.

Heartbroken.

She could handle being alone. She believed she could handle being without Mike. In fact, she knew she could. She'd done it for the last five years. The problem was that now that she'd gotten a taste of his love again and what it was like to spend time with him, she wanted to hold on to it. How could she go back to living life as she had before she ran into him at McCall Resorts' ribbon cutting ceremony?

Danielle curled upon her sofa with her head in her mother's lap. She alternated snatching tissues from the box on the coffee table, blowing her nose, and wiping her tears.

One thing she'd been grateful for was that her mom hadn't said, *I told you so.* That wouldn't have been of any use to her any way. She'd told herself so, yet that little voice couldn't stop her from doing what she thought was best, a win-win situation she convinced herself of.

With Every Moment

Danielle blew her nose again and choked back tears. She surprised herself that she still had more tears left after crying for the past hour. The last time she cried so much, her father had passed away.

She swallowed the rock in her throat and asked in a voice that even seemed foreign to her. "Mom, what can I do to make this right?"

"Give him time."

Not the answer she wanted. Nor the answer she believed would help. When she didn't respond, her mother continued, "When a man feels betrayed, it almost takes an act of God for him to forgive. They're stubborn, and their egos are fragile. And Mike is no different. But..." She paused for several seconds. Danielle could only assume she was searching for the right words or something to say to bring comfort. "Mike loves you, and deep down, he knows you love him too. He just needs a minute to digest all the surprises he's been thrown lately. I mean, can you blame him? He just found out that his real father is a man he never knew."

Danielle should have known better. Asking one question gave her mother license to spurt her opinion about everything. But she'd asked for this. And there was no one else she could talk to. Might as well let her talk. Share her opinions about Mike and his family.

"Now, I understand wanting the man to heal. But to have him staying in Thad's family's resort and spending Christmas with the man's family without telling him Thad was his father is over the top—too much without telling him the truth. Thad's identity was bound to come out in a way they hadn't planned. That's Soap Opera 101."

Danielle snickered.

As a child, she recalled her mom watching every soap opera that aired on television. Danielle had even watched a few episodes in college. Based on how things worked on television, Thad and Mabel withholding that crucial piece of information from Mike was doomed from the moment they decided they'd tell him when the time was right. Problem with that is they would've never gotten to choose that time. No matter what they told themselves.

"You might be on to something, Mom."

"Darn right I am." She rubbed Danielle's hair. "But I'm sorry things didn't work out the way you thought they would. Have you learned your lesson?"

"So many lessons."

Like, not taking money from strangers. Her mom taught her that when she was a kid, but somehow that didn't register when Thad made the offer.

Tell the truth, even when it might not be well received.

And to let love lead.

Thad's offer had been a quick fix to her financial woes. And as much as she needed that check, she had to give it back. She'd find a way to pay her mother's medical expenses, and she'd take out loans to finish law school.

Her ties to the McCall family would be severed once and for all.

CHAPTER FOURTEEN

Mike limped across the threshold of the McCall family mansion. When he made it through the foyer, his gaze darted toward the open kitchen area where he found Thad and Mabel watching him. Before their gazes locked, he felt them watching him. He'd been a bundle of confusion since Danielle's revelation.

He was no fool. He could understand how they must have thought they were doing the right thing for him, but their intentions didn't excuse their behavior or give them the right to meddle in his life.

They didn't flinch. It was as if they were poised for the inevitable conversation. Had they talked to Danielle? Did they know she'd told him everything? Whatever the case, the talk had to happen tonight. Now. No more secrets. No more hiding behind good intentions.

After all, good intentions were why they were standing there.

Mike made his way to where they stood. He pulled out the barstool he'd occupied yesterday—the same seat he sat in when he found out that Thad was his biological father. Perhaps that seat needed to go after today. He sat and watched the two of them for a while. They didn't speak, and neither did he. Mike linked his fingers and rested his forearms on the island top. He took several deep breaths to prepare for the conversation ahead. It was not his intent to be disrespectful, but by the end of their talk, he'd make it clear that he didn't want them meddling in his personal affairs. No matter the circumstances. And this was not the way for Thad to find a place in his life.

Mike measured his words and looked between the two of them. "Danielle told me everything."

Mabel peered through the open space. "And where is she now?"

"I sent her home. I don't want a fake fiancée or fake marriage. How could you two think any of this was appropriate?"

Mabel started to speak, but Thad spoke over her. "It was my idea. Since you'd lost your memory and Danielle was the first person you asked for coming out of surgery, I thought she would be our best bet to help you recover. Yes, my actions were selfish. I'd just found out about you, and if Danielle was our best and quickest hope, that's what I wanted. I hope you can understand that we asked the impossible of Danielle because we wanted to see you heal and regain your memory sooner than later."

"And of course she jumped at the opportunity when you threw your money in her face."

Mabel rushed to Mike's side. "No, no, no. Actually, Danielle had her reservations. She didn't think we were going about this the right way, but she went along with our plan because she loves you. In fact, she urged me and Thad to tell you the truth. She didn't want you to think what you think about her now. Please don't hold this against her. She truly loves you."

"I'm not sure if we can prove that she loves me or the check Thad signed and tossed her way."

With Every Moment

Every time the thought crossed his mind, Mike's chest burned with pain. He rested his forehead on his clenched fist. For the life of him, he couldn't wrap his mind around the fact that any of them thought this would work out for *his* good.

Mabel massaged his shoulder, then rested her head against it. "We didn't mean to cause you pain. We were only doing what we believed was in our power to do."

Mike swallowed the tightness in his throat. It didn't help because the tightness inflated his chest, made it difficult to breathe.

"Tell me, in your mind, how did you think this was going to end? For goodness' sake, y'all made me look like a fool, with me around here pressuring this woman about a wedding date." He chuckled and shook his head. "She must have thought I was out of my mind. But the crazy part about it is that she let me go on and on about wanting to get married as soon as possible—after Christmas, she said." Mike snorted at the memory.

He stopped talking for a moment. His wounded pride threatened to overtake him in the form of tears. How could they do this to him? No one seemed to comprehend the nightmare he starred in.

"We were supposed to set a wedding date after Christmas because she wanted to focus on my healing."

Mike turned to his mother. Her eyes shimmered. Surely, she sensed his pain, and for that reason alone, he wanted to cease his monologue. All his life, he aimed to please her, make her proud, but tonight, he had to express what she'd done to him.

"Momma, I'm disappointed in you. You had to know how I would feel about this arrangement when I found out. You knew how my relationship ended with Danielle five years ago and how that affected me. I just can't figure out why you, of all people, would think I'd find this okay."

Even if every second I spent with Danielle over the past week was a dream manifested.

"Of course I remember what happened between you two, but as your mother, I also saw how happy you were when you ran into her at McCall Resorts' grand opening. I also saw how your face lit up brighter than a Christmas tree when you saw her at the hospital. I was there at your side, and it was *her* you asked for. Not me."

Mike could see the disappointment that laced her eyes, but he couldn't quite be sorry for a memory he'd lost.

"Since the accident, you've been in a better mood than you've been since your breakup. So, yes, I thought Danielle was the solution. I'm sorry you didn't see it that way."

"It's hard to see Danielle as the solution when she stayed around to tick off her list of debts."

"It seems you've decided that you're going to see this from one side—through the lens of your pain—but know I'd make the same choice again. I think we all would. We were willing to do whatever it took to bring you back to us sooner."

"And if I never get my memory back? How long was she going to pretend?"

"Mike, the only thing that wasn't real was the relationship title. The love between you two is real, and eventually, if you never regained your memory, I think

171

marriage could've worked between you, but that seems to be a decision that no longer has to be made."

Thad remained quiet. And for that, he was thankful. Mike didn't know him well enough to consider his pleas, but he sensed Thad's sincerity. They were both thrown into a difficult situation. But Mike didn't grow up in a family who used their wealth to influence people and their decisions, so he couldn't say one way or the other if he would've made a similar choice as Thad.

But as a father, Thad's decision was extreme. Would his father, Victor, have done the same?

Mike pushed away from the island and stood with his palms pressed into the counter. Head down, he sucked in a chest full of air then released it to calm his nerves.

"While you all had your reasons for doing what you did, please don't let it happen again. And just so that we're clear, that means, don't interfere in my love life under any circumstances ever again. Period."

Because of them and this crazy television-influenced plan, he'd just lost the only woman he'd ever loved.

For good this time.

CHAPTER FIFTEEN

The tune of "Pomp and Circumstance" always gave Danielle chills.

Today, when the song started through the speakers, an overwhelming mix of emotions washed over her. From happiness because she'd accomplished her goal of completing law school to a sense of sadness. The sadness, however, she tried to shake off, but couldn't. It was as if the song signified the end of an era. And in a sense, it was. The end to her professional studies and the end to what she shared with Mike.

Four months, three weeks, and two days since they'd last spoken.

If there was any face she wanted to look into the crowd and see aside from her mother, it was his. But that was a dream. She didn't have the nerve to send him a graduation invitation, but secretly hoped the message would get to him through Nina.

The line of graduates began their march. Her fingertips grew cold. Her legs grew shaky with each step, and one lone butterfly fluttered in the pit of her belly.

Danielle marched down the aisle to her seat. Her eyes danced through the crowd hoping to spot her mother in the throng of spectators. She didn't find her, but she knew once her name was called, she'd spot her general vicinity from the shouting that would take place. Her mother always made sure she knew how proud she was of her achievements.

"Good morning, everyone. You may all be seated," Dr. Scott announced when each graduate filed into the room and stood in front of their chairs. The music stopped.

This is it.

Dr. Scott recognized the board of regents, university president, provost and vice president of academic affairs, and staff. "Today, we celebrate our resilient class, who have worked hard to get to where they are today. We salute you.

With Every Moment

Welcome to the hooding ceremony of Texas Southern University's Thurgood Marshall School of Law."

Everything else mentioned after that point was lost on Danielle. She got lost in the myriad of thoughts that centered on how she got to this point. For years, she'd been afraid to step out on faith and pursue her law degree. She'd settled for being Nina's personal assistant for almost eight years, though she wouldn't necessarily refer to it as settling. She'd learned so much from Nina. It was Nina who inspired her to go back to school and pursue her passions—to get her law degree. "I never want you to feel you need to stick around and babysit me," Nina had said on multiple occasions.

Danielle chuckled at the memory. She wouldn't call it babysitting. Nina had become like a sister to her. Scratch that. Nina was her sister. They'd grown close over the years. Nina had been the only person she could confide in and vice versa. They both grew up without siblings, and so they filled a void in both of their lives.

Danielle glanced around hoping to spot Nina. Though if she wasn't able to see her mother in the crowd, she'd probably miss Nina's face, too. She closed her eyes for a moment and imagined Nina giving her a thumbs up, followed by her encouraging smile. Her phone vibrated and broke her reverie.

We're so proud of you. Look to your left.

Danielle lifted her head toward the crowd on her left. Row by row, her eyes attempted to find a familiar face. Two pairs of hands waved in the air. Nina sat next to Bernadette. Andrew was there, too, holding their nine-month-old baby instead of waving with her mom and Nina.

And that was the extent of her support group.

For the life of her, she wasn't sure why she expected—well hoped—to see Mike's face. Expected that all was forgiven—or at least he'd see and understand that fake fiancée situation from her point of view. Not that she was asking him to agree, only understand that she stayed out of love, not the money.

But today was the start of her new life—a life he wouldn't be part of, and she had to be okay with that.

"God is good," the commencement speaker began. "God is good because I know it was only Him who guided you through the long days, and for some of you, sleepless nights."

Danielle chuckled. Her mind wandered off again. Yes, she had many sleepless nights. Some because of the work she'd put in to get this degree. Others because she wanted to call Mike. And others because she'd lie awake in bed wondering what he was doing and how life would be different if he were there to support her. She swiped at a lone tear.

Everyone on her row stood, and the classmate to her right tapped her shoulder. She snapped out of her reflections. Where had the time gone? With her thoughts focused on Mike and his whereabouts, she'd missed the invocation, the well wishes from a couple of professors who graced the stage, and even the encouraging remarks from the guest speaker.

Dear Lord, give me the strength to move on.

God was more than able to bring another man in her life when the time was right, but for now, this was the appointed time to get her new life on track.

Danielle stood in line alongside the stage and waited for her name to be called—well, more like teetered on the edge of bouncing from one foot to the other like she was about to jump in a boxing ring. She wriggled her fingers and took several breaths.

Settle down. I should not be this nervous.

"Danielle Alicia Adams, Juris Doctorate, magna cum laude."

There went the excessive screams from her little support section. Never mind the fact they were advised to hold their applause to the end. Of course her mother and Nina wouldn't listen. Danielle lurched forward and marched across the stage. She stopped in front of the cameraman, placed the hood around her neck, and posed. She strolled off the stage and waved to her mom and Nina, who snapped pictures with their camera phones. At least that's what she assumed they were doing. It was hard to tell what was happening with so many people in the audience.

After each name had been called, Dr. Scott returned to the stage. "Now, if you would all stand for the playing of the Texas Southern University alma mater. The program has the words on the back for those of you who would like to sing along with the instrumental."

When the music concluded, one of her classmates joined Dr. Scott on the stage to give the benediction. "Heavenly Father, we thank You for bringing us this far. We thank You for those You've placed in our lives to support us, mentor us, and guide us. I ask that You go before us and continue to guide our path, that we may honor You in wherever our journeys take us. In Jesus' name. Amen."

The graduates stood and marched out of the auditorium. Danielle posed for pictures, shared hugs, and congratulatory remarks with her classmates, especially those who were along the path she navigated to get to her mother and Nina.

Danielle locked eyes with her mother, rounding the corner with Nina, Andrew, and Andrew Jr. by her side. Her mother engulfed her in one of those I'm-proud-of-you hugs. Danielle fought to keep the tears from falling by holding her breath.

God, thank You for letting my mom live to see this day.

Because it almost didn't happen. Danielle didn't cash the check Thad had given her and prayed that they'd get some other miracle in return. Even though she still wanted to use the money, her mom refused the help. Her mom's word rang in her mind: "I've never seen the righteous forsaken nor his seed begging for bread. God will make a way, Danielle. Stop bearing this weight on your shoulders."

And He indeed made a way.

Not just for Danielle's mother, but for her as well. Thanks to prayers, her high LSAT scores, and her academic excellence, Danielle received a scholarship from Hudson & Stewart, LLP, a local law firm in the Houston area. The law firm agreed to pay her tuition as long as she committed to working with their firm after graduation.

She broke away from her mom and fell into Nina's arms. "I knew you could and would do it. I'm so proud of you. God is really showing out in your life—from the scholarship to graduation. When are you taking the bar?"

Nina released her, and she took a step back. Andrew patted her shoulder. "Congrats, Danielle. We're all proud of you."

"Thanks, Drew. Nina, I'm studying for the bar now. I've got plans to take it in July, so roughly two months left to get ready for it."

"Dang, girl. Breathe."

Her laser focus helped her keep her mind off Mike most days.

"I am. This weekend. Then I'm back on it. I don't want to take too much time off. I want to get to it while the knowledge is fresh."

Andrew Jr. squealed, as if he agreed. Danielle giggled. "See, Andrew Jr. understands."

"So what's next after you pass the bar?" Andrew asked.

"I plan to practice family law—child custody and adoption cases."

Nina wrapped an arm around Danielle's neck again. "With a heart like yours, perfect choice. Let's get outta here and get some brunch."

"Sounds good to me."

Nina and Danielle walked arm-in-arm into the parking lot with Bernadette, and Andrew walking behind with the baby cradled on his hip. Danielle released a heavy sigh. Whenever Nina linked arms with her and started a stroll, that was cue for Nina getting involved in her business.

"So I take it you decided against inviting Mike?"

"It's for the best."

"You sure about that? I know he misses you."

Danielle's heart escalated at the speed of a racehorse. "Did he say that?"

"Not necessarily, but I can see it in his face. He asks about you whenever I call to check in on him or the few times he's come to Atlanta to visit Thad."

"Oh, so they're working on their relationship. That's good."

Did that mean he'd find his way back to her? And didn't she just resolve to move on? Why did she care?

"Don't give up on him just yet is all I'm saying."

"Nina, you know I won't put my life on hold for him. He's had over four months to come around. I'm gonna focus on me. If he comes around, he'd just better hope I'm available."

"Is that so? You gonna get back with what's-his-name? You didn't care for Brandon that much anyway. If you ask me, you were looking for an out with him. Mike's accident was just convenient enough."

"Oh-kay," Danielle sang. "Enough about all of that. Let's just go eat and celebrate. Just no more Mike-related or relationship talk, okay?"

Nina saluted her. "You're the boss today so I won't press."

Who appointed her cupid anyway?

Ever since she and Andrew got married, Nina had been working to fix up anyone in her path. She and Andrew's mother, Rose, had success with Andrew's brother, Darius, and Kennedy. Now Nina had apparently set her sights on her. The only problem with that scenario was that she'd decided to move on.

And that's exactly what she planned to do.

CHAPTER SIXTEEN

Mike's saving grace: work.

He could depend on work to keep him busy.

Keep his mind off his problems.

Keep his mind off Danielle.

Throwing himself back into his normal routine—at least as normal as it could be since he still hadn't gotten his memory back—did the trick. His work as superintendent at SCI was the only way he knew to handle his stress. His bodily injuries had healed since the accident, so he lifted weights every now and again, but mostly worked overtime. Alcohol had never been something he enjoyed, so having a drink wasn't even on his radar. And as a man of faith, drowning his sorrows in the beds of different women went against everything he believed.

Five months, eight days, eleven hours.

That's how long it had been since he last saw Danielle's beautiful face or heard her voice. After several discussions with his mother, Kennedy, and even Thad, over the last five months, the hardness chipped away from his heart. With each passing day, he saw the situation from Danielle's point of view. Though it didn't excuse her from lying to him, his heart was now more receptive to what she had to say.

However, he couldn't bring himself to call her. Not yet. There was the situation with Thad that he'd been working through. He was still becoming used to the idea that his biological father wasn't Victor Stewart, the man he grew up emulating and adoring. But that made him love Victor even more. He stepped up and cared for him like he was his seed. Never treated him any different.

As he'd done since he got back to work, Mike walked through the doors at six-thirty. He'd given the excuse that he wanted to beat traffic and get a jumpstart on his day. Though those things were true, the issue was that he didn't sleep well most nights. Danielle's face graced and taunted his dreams. Contracts, permits, sketches, contractors, hard hats, flying debris, and the smell of wood, sheetrock, and fresh paint were the only things to help shift his focus.

SCI's clients benefitted from his diligence, even if everyone else in the office thought he needed to get a life.

As he'd done since he got back to work after the accident, Mike strolled into the office at six-thirty. First stop, breakroom for his morning cup of coffee. Cream, no sugar. Mike stood in front of the coffeemaker with his arms crossed over his chest, mentally running through his to-do list.

"I knew I'd find you here," Kennedy announced. She tapped his shoulder, and he thought he would jump out of his skin. He didn't scare easily, but he wasn't expecting anyone else to be in the office either. Even when Kennedy was working through her leadership issues last year, she didn't come in to work before seven.

Wait. How did I remember that?

"I wasn't expecting you here this early though. What's up?"

"I know you weren't, which is exactly why I'm here. You need an intervention."

Kennedy maneuvered around him so that she stood between him and the coffeemaker. She planted her hands on her hips, peered up at him, and squinted.

"Why am I picking up annoying little sister vibes from you?"

"Oh, you know why."

Mike rolled his eyes heavenward. He'd avoided the Danielle conversation with her for months now. He side-stepped her and retrieved his coffee mug.

"Don't tell me you rolled out of your bed early this morning to talk about my love life."

Kennedy hiked an eyebrow and moved to block his path. "So you know what this is about?" She thrust her palm in the air, daring him to move. "Just hear me out. When you two broke up before, I stayed out of it."

"As you should've."

"But, as your friend-like sister, I don't want to see you go down this path again, so I have to say something—at least try to talk some sense into you. Look, you've had your time to sulk, be angry, and run through all of your emotions, but do you really want to live the rest of your life without Danielle?"

"She made the choice for both of us when she decided that the only way she could stand to stay with me is if someone paid her to do it."

Kennedy twisted her lips in a scowl and folded her arms across her chest. "You can't honestly believe that money is the reason she stayed."

"The check she took from Thad says otherwise."

Kennedy threw her hands in the air. "I honestly can't believe we're having this conversation."

"I can't either. So why did you bring it up?"

"Because you need a smack upside your head, and I can't stand seeing you so unhappy."

"I am happy. I think our clients can agree with that. They're pleased with SCI's work."

"*Ugh.* You know I'm not talking about your work performance."

"Look at you...about to get married so you want to go around playing cupid. That's cute." Mike sipped his coffee and engaged Kennedy in a stare-down, a game they played as kids that he always won. They weren't kids anymore. He wouldn't allow anyone to make decisions about his love life. Not his mother. Not Thad. Not Danielle. And not Kennedy.

"What happened to you? When did you become so sarcastic? I want my friend-brother back."

Mike squeezed her shoulder and rested his hand there while he spoke. "Kennedy, I appreciate your concern, I honestly do, and I've handled the Danielle situation in the way I think is best. And I mean this is the nicest way possible. Please let me live my life and make my own decisions. I've had enough of my family thinking they know what's best for me." He pulled her into a hug and kissed her forehead.

"I understand. Just want you to have the love you deserve. You were a different man when she was around."

"So I heard. But thanks for looking out. I'll catch up with you later for our nine o'clock briefing."

Mike couldn't leave the breakroom fast enough. He believed he'd gotten to an emotional place where he was near ready to talk to Danielle, but after Kennedy cornered him, he wasn't so sure. He couldn't deny the fact that Danielle held his heart—that was never the issue. Could he ever trust her again? That's the question his heart couldn't answer.

He'd just about made it to his desk when Kennedy shuffled alongside him. "There's just one more thing. Two actually."

Mike sipped his coffee and peered at Kennedy through the slits in his eyes, but didn't break stride. "What's that?"

"I feel like you're trying to brush me off, but this is important, so I'll just wait until you take your seat."

Mike strolled into his office and took a seat in his executive leather office chair, which was a bit too fancy for his tastes, considering he mostly worked in the field, but it was something Kennedy insisted he have. "Alright. Let's hear it." He sipped his coffee then rested his back against the chair and laced his fingers across his abdomen. He didn't like that look in her eyes—a look that meant she was poised to ask for a favor, particularly one he might not like.

"I know I could have asked you this any other time, but now is just as good a time as any. I'd like for you to walk me down the aisle."

A wave of relief washed over him, and he relaxed his shoulders, a tension he didn't realize he held. An easy ask.

"Now you know that goes without saying. I think I would've been offended if you didn't ask."

Kennedy hurried around the desk and threw her arms over his neck. "Thanks so much, Ken." She jerked back. Tears sprang to her eyes. "I'm sorry. So sorry, Mike. I know you're not Ken. And I fully understand that it was you I asked. It's just that he's been on my mind so much lately. So many things he's missed and will miss, you know?" Kennedy said between tears.

Mike stood and hugged Kennedy until the tears subsided.

"I miss him, too, and I believe his spirit lives on through you. He's proud of you, Kennedy, just as much as I am. Hey, I'm your brother, too."

"I know." Kennedy backed out of his arms toward the door. "I'm sorry if you think I've been meddling in your life too much. Just want to see you happy."

"It's all good. I know your heart, sis."

The corners of Kennedy's lips turned upward into the kind of smile that told him he probably wouldn't like or agree with the second thing she wanted to talk with him about.

"I'm glad to hear that you know my heart because that also means that you understand that I'm fond of Danielle, and she's a friend to me."

Mike nodded, encouraging her to continue.

"So, I don't want you to be surprised if she accepts the invitation to attend my wedding."

Mike parted his lips, but Kennedy stopped him.

"I promise this has nothing to do with the two of you. I invited her because she's a friend. Just thought you should know so that you can prepare yourself however you need to do so." She backed closer toward the door. "See you at nine for our project meeting update."

Kennedy disappeared.

With Every Moment

Mike could hear his heart thumping in his ears. Seeing Danielle at the wedding—if she came—wouldn't be a problem. He'd speak and carry on. But what if he took one look in her eyes and decided that he, in fact, could not live without her—didn't want to live without her?

CHAPTER SEVENTEEN

Danielle stared at Darius and Kennedy's wedding invitation on her coffee table. For weeks, it taunted her. Made her belly churn, but also betrayed her and turned flips at the thought that she'd see Mike again if she attended. But was she ready to face him after he cast her away like a child sent to her room for punishment? The memory was fresh in her mind like it happened yesterday, but it also seemed like it was ages ago.

She picked up the invitation and reread the personal note from Kennedy.

I know you and Mike aren't on speaking terms, but I'd love it if you came to celebrate my new union with

Darius. Take all the time you need to decide, even if that means you can't make up your mind until the day of. Either way, I'll save a place for you.

XOXO, Kennedy

Kennedy didn't give her an option to back out. And what about Mike? Did he know about this open invitation? How did he feel about it? For starters, it wasn't his wedding, but she was ninety-nine percent sure he'd escort Kennedy down the aisle. Would her presence put him in a funk and ruin Kennedy's wedding day? No, Mike wouldn't do that to Kennedy, no matter what his feelings were about Danielle.

Still unable to make up her mind, Danielle tossed the invitation back on the tabletop and stretched her frame along the sofa. There were more pressing things on her to-do list, like taking the bar exam the next day. And taking her mother to the doctor for a checkup—praying that all was well and no major expenses would come.

Her thoughts drifted back to Thad's uncashed check. She kept it as a reminder that she didn't need his money to take care of her mom. And that vengeful part of her kept it— unsigned as proof she didn't mobile deposit it either—so that she could one day shove it into Mike's face to prove that she'd stayed around because she loved him. But what would that prove? And though the money influenced her actions in the beginning, it didn't hold the most weight.

Danielle picked up her cell phone and tapped and swiped until Nina's contact information appeared on the screen, but she hesitated to touch the talk icon. Talking with Nina always lifted her spirits, but with Kennedy's impending wedding, the conversation would eventually lead to whether Danielle would attend, and she hadn't made her mind up about it. She placed the phone back on the table.

Though happy for Kennedy, Danielle couldn't push aside the thought that she could've been in Kennedy's shoes right now. Nor could she erase the fact that she'd have to encounter Mike to seal the fate of their relationship, or lack thereof, once and for all.

∞

Self-care.

Her last semester of law school had been the most stressful time in her life. Late nights and early mornings. Endless hours of studying. Loads of caffeine. Little time to spend with her mom or chatting with Nina. Perhaps the breakup with Mike was a blessing in disguise, if she could even call it a breakup since they weren't in an actual relationship. Whatever the case, she had to maintain her sanity. And one way she learned to care for herself was through the practice of yoga.

Yoga helped her find her inner peace, flexibility, let go of anger, and accept the person God created her to be. On especially stressful days, she completed two sessions. Today would be one of those days. The Texas Uniform Bar Exam was administered over a two-day period. With the first part scheduled to begin in two hours, she prepared her mind with her favorite stretches. With each movement and concentration of breath, she celebrated all she had become and all that would come because of her passing the test.

She turned on the television and navigated to her fitness app. She chose her favorite release and placed her yoga mat on the floor. She completed the release enough times that she knew all the instructor's motivational quotes. She imagined the instructors, Diana and Kylie, knew today was a big day for her and cheered her on with their inspiring phrases.

Yes. Today would be a great day.

After her last stretch and moment of relaxation and meditation, Danielle's phone vibrated. She turned off the television and grabbed her phone to check the messages. Three encouraging her to do well—her mom, Nina, and Kennedy. She hadn't spoken with Kennedy to tell her about the test. She was sure she had Nina to thank for that. There was no telling what kind of scheming Nina had been up to behind her back, but today wasn't the day to be concerned about that.

Danielle responded to the texts, then set her phone to silent. She showered and dressed like she would if she were going to take the test somewhere else other than her home computer. Though she didn't like the idea of a virtual exam, the idea of avoiding Houston traffic appealed to her and her nerves.

She flipped open her Bible to the read specific Scriptures she'd marked for this occasion. *Be anxious for nothing…All things work together for the good of those who love God and are called according to His purpose...Do not be afraid, do not be discouraged. For the Lord your God is with you wherever you go...For I know the plans I have for you declares the Lord...*

An overwhelming sense of peace washed over her entire being.

Her heart steady.

Her fingers no longer jittery.

Her mind at ease.

Time to give it everything she had.

∞

Finally free. After two days of the most intense examination in her life, Danielle could breathe. It was as if she carried around a weight that had been lifted. She crossed the finish line.

She hadn't laid eyes on her mom in two weeks because her face had been buried in study material. Danielle navigated her car into a parking space outside of the senior living center where her mom lived. She tripped, but balanced herself using one-foot acrobatic moves, which kept her from falling. *Thanks, yoga. Slow down.*

A combination of cinnamon, lavender, and lemon assaulted her senses when she walked through the sliding glass doors. It was a smell her stomach couldn't take, but didn't bother her mother, and that was all that mattered. She locked eyes with her mother who sat in one of the lobby guest chairs hugging her purse to her chest. Was she late? Danielle flipped her wrist to check the time. In the five years Bernadette had lived in the senior living community, she'd never waited on Danielle in the lobby, and that change made Danielle's scalp tingle.

Danielle rushed to her side and kneeled.

"Mom, is everything okay?"

"Yeah, it is. I should ask you that, running in here like someone is chasing you with a pitchfork."

She chuckled. "Really, Mom? I guess I just thought something might be wrong. You never wait for me in the lobby."

"And that means something is wrong? Why didn't you think that maybe I'm ready to leave? Or that maybe I missed my only girl who I haven't seen in weeks."

Danielle leaned closer, squeezed her neck, then kissed her cheek. "Let's go with the latter."

She held out her hand, and Bernadette took hold of it. She steadied herself to stand, shifting more of her weight on Danielle than she anticipated. "C'mon. Let's go see what your physical therapist has to say."

This is what she'd been missing—human connection, mother-daughter connection. She'd been locked away in her home studying for so long that she'd forgotten what it felt like. Her heart warmed from the closeness.

They spent the entire twenty-five-minute drive to the physical therapist's office rehashing Danielle's experience from sitting for the Uniform Bar Examination. Though an experience she believed she'd properly prepared for and was glad she'd put behind her, she'd much rather focus on her mother's upcoming appointment. If she never spent another second in any medical facility, outside of a routine checkup, she'd be just fine. Over the past few years, she'd seen the inside of doctor's offices and hospitals enough that she knew the precise paint used on the walls and the color flooring. She'd seen enough.

"Even though I feel like I did everything I could do to prepare, my anxiety was on ten. But that could've been because it was a timed test. You know how I feel about timed tests."

"Don't I know it? You broke out in hives when you took your first state test in elementary school."

They chuckled at the memory.

"Poor Ms. Williams almost had a heart attack."

"I know. I think she may have panicked more than me, but thank goodness it wasn't anything like that over the past two days. I got through it alright because even though I had a bout of anxiety, I also had this overwhelming sense of peace—like everything would be alright. So I worked to keep my mind there."

"You've always done well, Dani, and I'm sure even that ol' bar exam can't stand up to you. I'm just happy I lived long enough to see it happen."

Every organ inside of Danielle clenched. She couldn't stand it when her mother mentioned her mortality. The thought of her not being around and leaving her in this world without a mother was more than she wanted on her mind at any point in time. More times than she could count, she'd asked her mom not to talk like that, and her response had always been the same: "Well, Dani, we all have to go someday. We just have to be sure we've straightened out our business with the good Lord before it's too late."

Danielle turned into the physical therapist's office parking lot, navigated into an empty space, and shifted the gear into park. Instead of asking her mom not to speak of her mortality, she said, "Okay, we're here. Can we pray before we go in?"

"You don't even have to ask." Bernadette took her hand.

Danielle prayed, "Father God, we honor You today. We come into Your holy presence to say thank You for all that You've done. Thank You for your new mercies and grace. And again, we thank You for making a way so that the medical bills will be covered. Thank You for a successful hip replacement. You've been so good to us, and we just ask that You keep my mom in good health, that we receive a good report in the next few minutes. In Jesus' name. Amen."

Danielle had to fight back rising thoughts of Thad's offer to pay her mom's medical expenses if she pretended to be Mike's fiancée and Mike's response to everything that happened. This moment wasn't about them. It was about her mother, and she worked doubly hard to keep her heart and mind focused.

∞

Tears of happiness streamed down both Danielle and her mother's faces. Three months after her hip replacement surgery, and all was well. Her physical therapist was pleased with her progress and didn't need to see her again until next year, unless problems occurred.

Danielle drove them to Snooze A.M. Eatery for brunch after her mother's appointment. After they sat and placed their orders for omelets and hash browns, Danielle became uneasy under her mother's gaze. For the past ten minutes, she had this wide-eyed look like she wanted to say something, but wasn't sure if she should. It was the same look she gave Danielle when she decided she wanted to live in a senior living facility after Danielle's father died. Her mom had never been one to not say what was on her mind, so whatever was bothering her had to be serious.

Danielle squared her shoulders and braced her core. "What is it, Mom? I thought we were celebrating."

The waitress returned with Danielle's latte and her mother's coffee. Her mother doctored up her drink with cream and sugar.

"Now that I'm all taken care of, what about you?"

Danielle sipped her latte. "What do you mean?"

"Kennedy's wedding is coming."

"How'd you know about the wedding?"

"I received an invitation. It seems I'm family now, after spending Christmas with the McCalls." She sipped her coffee and watched Danielle over the brim of her mug.

Danielle nodded. "I see."

"You planning to go?"

Danielle shrugged and sipped her latte again. "Not sure yet. I don't think Mike wants me there."

"Well, it ain't his wedding, is it?"

"But he'll be there."

"And what does that have to do with anything since you said it's over between you two? Are you saying it isn't really over?"

"Mom, he was pretty clear the last time I saw him. Besides, I don't want it to look like I'm there to see him. It's best not to rehash emotions. We're better off letting things stay the way they are, and the best way to do that is for me to steer clear. I'll send her a gift, though."

Did she even believe the words that came out of her mouth? She sounded convincing, even to herself, yet she wasn't sure if the way things were was the way she wanted them to be.

"Hmmph."

"What is that supposed to mean?" *Why did I even ask?*

She'd just given her mother permission to give her opinion about her love life. The tiny hairs on her arms stood. Her stomach tightened. Even her body knew that was a bad idea. Too late to take it back now.

"I know you don't really want my opinion, but I'm going to give it to you anyway. Mike is the kind of guy who wears his heart on his sleeve. He may have felt betrayed, but his love for you is still there. I watched the two of you on Christmas. That man would move the world for you if he could. He was the same way five years ago. I think he just needs some time to process everything that happened after the accident. You know…the way you and his parents handled things. And even if it really is over, it's best that y'all talk it out and really move on."

"Who says I haven't moved on?"

Her mother shot her one of those you-can't-be-serious looks. She sipped her coffee and fixed her gaze on Danielle, and Danielle did everything she could not to look her mother in the eye. One close look, and she'd be able to confirm everything she said was true. Danielle focused on her near-empty cup of latte.

"So, what's it gonna be? I didn't raise you to be a coward, Dani."

"I'm not a coward."

"Well, put your big girl panties on and stop trying to run from the situation. Face it, and move on."

Bernadette reached across the table and lifted Danielle's chin with her finger.

"I mean it, baby girl. Whatever your choice is, make it, and make it clear to him. What's the new term now? Level up?" She laughed. "You're levelin' up in everything else. Do it with your relationships, too."

Danielle chuckled at her terminology. It didn't sound the same coming from her mother. She fought back the tears that threatened to fill her eyes. She hadn't wanted to face the situation. At least this way, there was still an inkling of a chance that they'd find each other again. But to mutually decide it was over—for the second time and probably for good this go 'round—she wasn't ready for that.

"Now what time are you picking me up for this wedding?"

"I'm not sure what time it starts. I'll have to check the invitation."

Danielle knew the wedding started at two o'clock. She'd picked up the invitation at least fifty times. She could practically recite every word plus the personal note from Kennedy. And Danielle was no fool. Surely Kennedy invited

Bernadette as an extra push to get Danielle to come—a final matchmaking attempt on her part. Nina was probably involved, too.

The waitress arrived with their food. The smile that graced her mother's face was one that said, "My job here is done." It was time to end—or begin—this thing with Mike, once and for all.

CHAPTER EIGHTEEN

Slowly, Mike allowed Thad into his life. A little over seven months ago, Mike found out Thad was his biological father. That had taken some getting used to. Actually, he was still getting used to the idea. Since then, Mike talked on the phone with Thad here and there, with Thad initiating most of their contact. Thad made trips back to Houston to visit with Mike and Mabel. Though Thad insisted he was interested in getting to know Mike, he spent more time with Mabel. But Mike couldn't blame Thad for that. A part of him still held on to his displeasure regarding Thad's dealings with Danielle. Thad understood and promised to give him time to heal.

And it wasn't that he didn't like Thad as a person. He seemed kind enough. He lavished his mother with attention.

Called her often. Sent her flowers. Treated her with respect. And he treated her like she was the only woman in his world who mattered. It was easy to see why she'd fall for him…again.

But, he promised his mom and himself that he'd make an honest effort.

Mike navigated his car down the winding path that led to McCall Resorts. Thad had flown into town for the weekend for father-son bonding activities. Mike planned to spend most of the day at the resort with him. The closer he got to the main house, memories from the last time he was there flooded his mind. Christmas Day. With Danielle. He missed her, but fear kept him from picking up the phone to call. What if she didn't really love him as she claimed while she pretended to be his fiancée? Mike shook his head to rid himself of the negative thoughts. He didn't doubt her love for him. He only questioned if he could trust her with his heart.

Mike parked in the semi-circle driveway in front of the main house. By the time he climbed out of the car and rounded the bumper, the front door opened. Thad's frame filled the doorway, looking like he belonged on the cover of *PGA* magazine, dressed in a matching hat and polo shirt with khaki shorts that mirrored Mike's look.

"Hey, Mike." Thad pulled him into a quick hug and slapped his back.

"Hey. What's up? You've been spying on me or something?" Mike flicked Thad's sleeve. They were both wearing green shirts and matching hats.

"I may or may not have had my people check to see what you were wearing and report back."

They shared a chuckle.

Thad added, "Ready to play eighteen?"

"About as ready as I'll ever be."

Golf would never be his first-choice sport, but because it would take a few hours, that would give them time to talk without his mom being around. Good ol' quality man-to-man, getting-to-know-each-other time. Mike had learned the sport with his late friend, Kendrick, to network with current and prospective SCI clients back when Kendrick first started SCI.

"Darius and Kennedy are inside talking wedding stuff. You want to come in and talk with them before we take off?"

"Yeah. I'll do that."

Mike strolled past Thad through the foyer, the wood flooring quiet beneath his feet. Even though the holidays had long passed, that cozy family feeling lingered in the massive house. A whiff of apple cinnamon teased his senses, a sure reminder of the fresh apple pie he'd enjoyed when he stayed over during the Christmas holidays. And although Darius occupied the house, there was a feminine touch to it. Fresh flowers in crystal vases sat on each end table in the sitting room. There were even those throw pillows Kennedy liked. He smirked and continued his trek to the kitchen where Kennedy and Darius sat in his direct line of vision.

"Getting cold feet yet?"

Kennedy and Darius looked over their shoulders and smiled.

Darius pounded his fist against Mike's. "Nah, man. I can't wait to make her my wife." He reached over and squeezed Kennedy's hand. If he ever had any doubt about

213

the way Darius felt about Kennedy, it washed away when he witnessed the way he looked at her.

"None here, either. Just a few more weeks left. We're done with marriage counseling. My house is already on the market. Most of my things are packed up. Ain't nothing to it but to do it."

Mike wrapped Kennedy in a bear hug. "So happy for you, sis. You deserve all the happiness in the world."

Kennedy pulled out of his embrace and reclaimed her seat on the barstool next to Darius.

"Thanks, Mike. So you're off to dust off your golfing skills, I hear."

"Yeah, something like that. I might let him win since it's our first time playing together."

"I heard that," Thad called out from the family room.

Mike chuckled. "I just came to speak. I'll catch up with y'all later. Take care of her, D."

"Already done."

Kennedy blurted, "So still no plus one for the wedding, Mike?"

His heart constricted. "Don't you start."

She shrugged. "What? It was an innocent question. We're making final seating arrangements this week. Just wondering if I should leave a space open next to you, that's all."

Nothing was innocent about that question. That was Kennedy's side-handed way of asking about Danielle. The thought of having her next to him as he celebrated Kennedy, who was like a sister to him, was a nice idea. But, they weren't on speaking terms. For a sliver of a second, he wondered if she'd accept the invitation if he called. He hated what that fake fiancée situation did to him. He'd never questioned himself around her before—sucked that he had to look over his shoulder when it came to her now.

"I think you know the answer to your question, but I'll say it again: No plus one. My focus is on getting you down the aisle. Just let me know what you need, and I got you. Don't worry about me. I'm good."

Mike leaned in and kissed her forehead.

Kennedy twisted her lips and tapped her chin. "*Hmmm.* We'll see about that."

Mike rolled his eyes heavenward and left to join Thad in the family room. "About ready for tee time, old man?"

"We'll see if you're singing the same tune when I finally break ninety today."

Mike shrugged and pressed his palm into his chest. "Ouch. I'm not the best, but I'm sure I can beat you by a few shots. Care to make a friendly wager?"

Thad rubbed his thumb and forefinger under his chin. "What are you willing to lose?"

Mike chuckled and thought for a moment. He had nothing left to lose. "Loser buys dinner."

"I can live with that. Let's roll. Our golf cart is waiting for us outside."

Mike called over his shoulder to Kennedy and Darius. "Later guys."

Thad walked ahead and picked up his golf bag, waiting in the foyer. Mike followed Thad out the door and retrieved his golf bag from his trunk before he joined Thad in the golf cart.

With Every Moment

An upside to not being able to recall the last five years of his life—and according to his doctor, he likely wouldn't regain his memories at this point—was he got to experience the resort with new eyes. Thad drove the golf cart, and Mike took in the scenery: the lush greenery on both sides of the road, lodging designed like mini castles, gourmet restaurants, and the different activities were a sight to see. All he could think was that Kennedy was moving on up. Why would she even want to continue working at SCI knowing that she was marrying into a life of luxury? His bet: to honor Ken's memory.

Thad pulled into the parking lot of the modern two-story golf facility.

"Mr. McCall, Mr. Stewart, welcome to McCall Resorts Club. I'm Peter, and I'll be around to assist you with anything you need today. Will you be requiring the assistance of a caddy this afternoon?"

Thad looked to Mike, who shook his head. He always carried his own clubs. "Thanks, Peter, but I think we'll handle them ourselves today."

"That's fine." Peter handed them a card. "Just call this number if there's anything you need while you're on the course. Please follow me to get you checked in."

Peter led them into the golf club, which was fancier than any Mike had ever been to. The club had two penthouses that were available to be used by members and their guests. The interior and exterior walls were made from Travertine imported from Portugal. And the limestone flooring was imported from Peru. Facts that Mike wasn't sure how he knew. On the way to check in, they passed the MRC store, a sports bar with several large-screen televisions, and a restaurant that made him feel like he needed to bring a jacket and tie if he wanted to dine there.

This would be a fine way to schmooze SCI's clients.

Peter stopped and rounded a counter and tapped a few keys on a computer. Mike's attention shifted to a familiar face walking through the club. He blinked several times, wondering if his vision failed him.

Peter broke his train of thought when he said, "Good to go. Anything else I can assist you with?"

"We've got it from here, Peter. We'll call if we need you."

"Alright then. Give me a ring if there's anything I can do to make your visit more pleasurable. We already have water and ice in the cooler on the golf cart. Would you like any beer to add to the cooler?"

"No thanks, Peter. We're all good."

Thad and Mike left the check-in area and retraced their steps back out to their cart.

"Nervous yet?"

"Not in the slightest, but I sense some hesitation on your part, so I'll go easy on you."

Mike laughed. "Yeah, go ahead and set yourself up now so you can use that excuse when we finish the last hole."

When they made it back to the cart and reclaimed their seats, Mike turned to Thad. "So is this how the rich live, or is Peter that hospitable to everyone?"

"I think there are perks when it's your family who owns the resort. Wouldn't want the family to have a bad experience, right?"

"True that. Man, was that HV3 I saw in there?"

Harold Varner III was one of a handful of African American golfers who played on the PGA tour. Though Mike didn't consider himself a die-hard golf fan, he kept up with the careers of golfers like HV3 and Tiger Woods.

"Yeah. He's probably just getting ready for the upcoming tournament—the annual Labor Day PGA Fundraising Event is coming up next month. In the past, the resort has held it in Georgia, but since this location is new, they're holding it here this year. Proceeds will go to the Texas Children's Hospital."

"Nice."

Mike hadn't expected to see pro golfers around, but wouldn't say that surprised him, considering the luxurious vibe of the resort.

Thad navigated the cart to the driving range. They spent a few minutes warming up and practicing their swings.

After thirty minutes of warm-up, Mike was ready. They hopped back in the cart, and Thad drove them to the first hole. They climbed out of the cart, and Mike pulled the bib of his hat down and folded his arms across his chest. "You first."

With Every Moment

Thad stepped up to the tee and hit a beautiful drive off it. He and Mike watched as his ball fell short of the first bunker, about two hundred fifteen feet away. Mike followed and outdrove Thad about thirty feet as he cleared the bunker and landed in the center of the fairway. At the end of the first hole, Mike birdied, and Thad missed the putt to finish at par.

"You think Tiger will win another one?" Thad asked.

"Definitely. He's still got it."

"Yeah, I agree. It'd be nice to watch him play."

"Will he be here for the fundraiser tournament?"

"Nah, not this one, but maybe next time."

"With the way your life is set up, I'm surprised you haven't met him already."

Thad chuckled. "I'm not the rich one. My brother is."

"Could've fooled me."

For the front nine, Mike scored better than Thad for more than half of them, though he was sure the light winds helped him out.

"You've got more skills than I thought. I can't take it easy on you anymore."

Mike laughed. "Is that what you were doing?"

"I can show you better than I can tell you. Just watch me on the back nine."

Their conversation had mostly been light banter, for which Mike had been thankful. However, there was something that bothered him since he found out about Thad's relationship to him and his mother. Thad drove them to the tenth hole and climbed out of the cart. Another cart pulled up alongside them with drinks and snacks. They accepted and took a moment to finish them before they resumed their game.

"I've been thinking a lot about all that's happened. My mom has told me her side of the story, but I want to hear yours. If you loved her so much, why didn't you ever look for her?"

Something in Thad's demeanor changed, like he'd been waiting on Mike to ask him something personal. He leaned against the cart and looked Mike in the eyes, though he wasn't really looking at him. His eyes held this far-away glint, like his mind had gone back in time.

"Times were different almost forty years ago, as you can imagine. No cell phones or internet. I looked for her as much as I could. I went back to her house in Atlanta to look for her, and all her mother told me was she wasn't there and that she wasn't coming back. I wrote letters and sent them to her grandmother's house, but they were returned. I figured that was my best bet because she visited her every summer when we were in high school. When that didn't work, I didn't know what to do. I gave up, but I never stopped loving her. Mabel has always had my heart. Never met another woman like her."

"So you never got married?"

"I did, after I finished medical school. Cheryl died in a car accident five years after we were married. I sorta had a case of déjà vu when I found out about you, and moments later, you were involved in an accident. I didn't want to risk losing you and I'd just learned you were my son. I couldn't save Cheryl, but I could help you. I had to do whatever I could. And because of everything that followed, Danielle seemed like the best solution to help you pull through. I know you didn't care for that, but I'd do it all over again if it means it'll help you even a little bit."

Mike never really considered what drove Thad to his decision to interfere in his life the way he did. Knowing what he'd gone through with his first wife, he understood why Thad made the decisions he did—including paying Danielle to help in his recovery. His heart must've gotten the message because it created an abnormal erratic rhythm when Thad mentioned Danielle. Oh, how he missed her, but there was still this miniscule piece of him that wanted to hold on to the hurt.

"And there hasn't been anyone else after Cheryl?"

Mike moreso searched for an inkling of hope that he'd find someone else if he couldn't bring himself to see Danielle again. Would he be one of those people who felt like there was only one person in the world for him and regret it later in life?

"I've dated many other women. Most of them were beautiful inside and out—just missing that special something. When you've loved and have been loved so deeply, it's hard to settle for anything else once you know what it feels like. Not many people get to experience it."

That's what I'm afraid of.

"And the trouble with staying in a relationship when a woman loves you more than you love her is that sooner or later, she realizes it and leaves you anyway. You can't have one foot in the door—at least that was the story with me and Liz. She left me a few months before I came to Houston for the grand opening."

"Sorry to hear that."

His heart ached. The tightening in his chest pained him at the thought of his life turning out that way because he couldn't give his and Danielle's relationship another chance.

"Thanks, but I tell you I believe the good Lord had mercy on me 'cause when I walked through that door and saw Mabel, every word of that saying came alive to me. You know the one: When God closes one door, He opens another one. One look at her, and I knew I never stopped loving that woman. I just hate that we've missed out on so much time. Sorry I wasn't there for you."

It was time to end this conversation. Mike blinked a few times. The back of his eyes stung, and he didn't like it one bit.

"It was beyond your control. C'mon. Let's finish this back nine so you can buy me dinner."

Thad slapped him on the back and walked across the Bermuda grass to take his first swing at the tenth hole. Mike kept the conversation lighter from that point, learning more about who his mom was in her teens and early twenties. Thad won the game, but still bought dinner for the two of them. Though he had his doubts in the beginning, Mike thought highly of Thad, and though he may not have intended to, he helped Mike put his feelings about Danielle into perspective. He didn't exactly have a plan for how he would go about reconciling with her, but allowing forty years to go by without speaking to her was out of the question.

CHAPTER NINETEEN

Danielle stood before the floor-length mirror and shifted her stance from front to side then to rear. She'd changed in and out of three dresses. At first, she thought she'd go with a pink dress she'd bought to match the wedding colors, but she didn't care for how the dress fit her frame. Then there was the black dress that was perfect, but she decided against it, resolving that she was on her way to a wedding and not a funeral. And last was the emerald one-sleeve knee-length dress that accentuated all of her curves. Like the black dress, it was perfect, except she'd worn that dress on a date with Mike years ago. Would he think she wore it to get his attention? Better yet, would he even remember it?

Her bedside clock decided for her. If she changed again, she'd be late, and that would be tacky and rude. Plus, she still had to pick up her mom.

She slipped into a pair of black pumps and smoothed her hands along the front of the dress. "This will have to do."

Her heart drummed in sync with her steps on the way to her car, revved up along with the engine, and pumped as fast as the wheels spun. When she reached the first stoplight, she leaned over and rummaged through her glovebox for a napkin or dried-up wipe to clean the steering wheel and her sweaty palms. Running her palms along her dress again was not an option. Thankfully, she found a crumbled-up napkin from a fast-food restaurant. She sniffed it before wiping her hands with it, then the steering wheel.

The light turned green. Danielle accelerated and pulled in a deep breath. She released it slowly and practiced the breathing techniques she'd picked up in yoga class. She hadn't seen Mike in almost eight months. In fact, today made exactly eight months since they last had any communication. She'd gone longer without seeing him, so why was she losing her wits now?

Smile. Have a good time. You can get through this. Do unto others as you would have them do unto you.

And what would that be in this situation? She wanted to love him as much as she wanted to shove that check in his face to prove that love was her ulterior motive, not money. But what good would that do? Would such an action keep them apart for another eight months? Or longer? That wasn't what she wanted. Sure, she could prepare her heart and mind for seeing him again today, but none of that would do her any good when she laid eyes on him. She chuckled to herself. Her mother would have all the unsolicited answers.

Fifteen minutes later, she arrived at the senior living community.

Okay. Today is not about you and Mike. It's about Kennedy and Darius.

And she'd remind herself of that fact as often as possible, and doubly when she set eyes on Mike.

Once again, her mom was waiting for her in the lobby. When she saw Danielle, she stood, shimmied her shoulders, and spun around to show off her outfit.

"Mommy, you look so nice in that jumper. You'll practically have to get undressed just to go to the restroom though."

"I didn't even think about that." She chuckled. "I was only concerned with how good I looked."

"And that canary yellow is gorgeous on you."

"You look beautiful, too. Are you trying to take the spotlight from the bride, get that man's attention, or both?"

"Now you cut that out." Danielle waved her toward the exit. "Come. Let's get out of here."

They avoided the Mike conversation during the forty-minute drive to the resort. Danielle's muscles relaxed, and for that moment, she could take her mind off the what-ifs concerning him.

Danielle entered the resort and drove to the main house. At the driveway entrance, valet drivers were on standby to park the guests' cars. She shifted the gear into park, and a short bald-headed gentleman dressed in all black with a red vest rushed to the car and greeted her.

"Good afternoon. Welcome to the McCall wedding. Here's your pickup ticket."

Her mom climbed out of the car and met her in front of it. "See, this is some real rich people stuff right here. I ain't mad at 'em."

Danielle chuckled and shook her head.

Pink-and-green flower petals guided them to an oversized clear tent with flower-covered chandeliers. As if the resort wasn't already a paradise, the tent setup made Danielle feel like she was on an island. The chair coverings were white with pink-and-green flowers. Danielle mused Darius must really love Kennedy to agree to that. A sentiment that made those tiny goosebumps pop up along her arms, probably because it was the kind of thing Mike would do for her—at least he would have over five years ago.

Hardwood flooring covered the grass. String lights hung from corner to corner. Love songs that reminded her of her old college days played softly, setting the atmosphere. With only twenty chairs for guests, this was scheduled to be an intimate event.

"This is gorgeous, Mom."

"Sure is. Hope I live long enough to see you get married."

Danielle thrust a finger in the air. "*Uh-uh.* We will not talk about my love life today. This is Kennedy's day." She'd been thinking the same thing, so she verbalized that moreso to remind herself than to remind her mother.

"Just saying that I'm getting older. Just one of the things I like to do before I die—have grandkids, too."

Danielle gave her the side eye. "Don't cut up today, Momma. Remember what happened the last time we were here?"

"Now, that wasn't my fault. I wasn't the one lying to him. And I must not have showed out too much, I'm considered family and received a wedding invitation." With that, she strolled ahead and took a seat on the second row on the bride's side.

Danielle shook her head, marched behind her, and took her own seat.

Fifteen more minutes left before the ceremony was scheduled to begin. In the next several minutes, the remaining guests arrived. She recognized Thad and his brother, Jeffrey McCall, from the grand opening. They exchanged waves and smiles. Thad checked his watch then shuffled over to join her and her mom.

"How've you beautiful ladies been?"

"Good," they echoed together.

Danielle gave her best please-don't-mention-Mike smile. "Thanks for asking. What about you?"

"Things are definitely looking up. Mike is coming around, so that's all I could ask for."

She fought to keep a neutral face at the mention of Mike's name, but evidently she failed because he added, "I think he's come around regarding you, too. He'll be glad to see you here today."

If that were the case, why hasn't he called? And if he did, would I have answered? There was this small selfish part of her that wanted him to feel the same heartache she endured when he made her leave the park last year.

She stuttered and tumbled out, "I'm glad things are going well for the two of you."

"You're a fine young lady, Danielle. Mike knows what he has in you." He winked and returned to his seat.

See, that was exactly the conversation, pep talk, or whatever he wanted to call it, she didn't need. Now she had to push back that combination of apprehension and anticipation—control her emotions before they ran rampant.

Danielle turned to her mother who remained quiet with a smile plastered on her face.

"You're a little too quiet for comfort. You have no comment about Thad's mentioning of Mike?"

"He wasn't talking to me. He was talking to you. What comments do you have?" She hiked that knowing motherly eyebrow.

Danielle slid back in her seat and faced the flower-covered wedding arbor. "None. None at all."

"Ummm-hmmm."

A woman in a maxi-length dress that coordinated with the pink flowers strutted up to Thad and Jeffrey. Danielle couldn't read her lips, but whatever she said made them get up and leave with her. Based on the headset and professional demeanor, Danielle assumed her to be the wedding coordinator.

With Every Moment

Minutes later, the wedding singer's voice rang through the tent with the worship song, "How Deeply I Need You." That song always made Danielle reflect on her relationship with God, and today helped set the tone for the path the newlyweds desired to take—keeping God first in their marriage. The lyrics also shifted Danielle's heart. Made her focus less on seeing Mike and more on seeing God at work in the lives of the bride and groom. Her heart settled. She relaxed more in her seat. This was far bigger than anything going on between the two of them.

When he finished that song, the pianist's fingers seamlessly went into the next song—one she recognized before he parted his lips. Her heart and mind went straight into mush mode when the lyrics to Brian McKnight's "Still in Love" flowed from his lips. The wedding party entered, which left little space for her to think about herself, thank goodness.

Darius, his brother and best man, Andrew, along with the minister walked into the tent and stood at the wedding arch. Thad walked Mabel down the aisle. Her dress was much like the color of the wedding coordinator, but much more flattering and perfect for the August heat. She stood in as Kennedy's mother. He escorted her to the seat in front of Danielle and her mom. Jeffrey and Rose walked down the aisle next. Her dress was an apple green. A sheen glistened as she walked in the sheath dress. Though simple, Danielle sensed it was expensive. The fabric didn't look like anything she pulled off the rack at a department store. Her eyes were glossy, yet happy. She wore the smile of a proud mom. They took the front-row seats on the opposite side of the tent.

Nina glided down the aisle along with Andrew Jr. in one arm and a single long-stemmed rose in the other. Andrew Jr. wasn't too concerned about his role as ring bearer. He held the ring pillow in his fists, making a show of jerking around in Nina's arms to gnaw on it. The guests chuckled. He took his cue from the giggles because he bucked and moved even more. When she made it to the wedding arch, she handed the baby to Rose and stood to the left of the men.

The wedding singer began "Endless Love." After the first line, another singer entered the tent and continued the duet. Kennedy and Mike appeared at the door of the tent, and the guests stood. *Ooh*s and murmurs of how stunning Kennedy looked echoed throughout the tent. The strapless mermaid wedding dress looked like it was designed especially for her. Her face was framed with a gorgeous, yet hesitant smile. Danielle knew her well enough to know that the attention made her uncomfortable for a moment. Mike leaned over and whispered something into her ear. Her smile brightened, her back straightened, and she stood there a moment longer, posing for pictures, though her eyes were glued to the man at the end of the aisle.

∞

"This is your day. You only get one of these, so enjoy it. Darius is waiting for you to be his forever. I'll miss you, but I trust he's got you." Mike's throat tightened as he uttered the words to Kennedy. Though they weren't blood relatives, they'd practically grown up that way. Knowing he would give her away to another man on behalf of her father and brother made the moment even more emotional.

Kennedy's tear-filled eyes looked up at him.

"Don't cry now. You'll ruin that makeup."

She released a soft chuckle.

"I'm sure they would all be proud of you and the choice you made. Your mom, dad, Ken—all of them. Mom and I are proud, too. You got this, girl."

She accepted the encouragement and nodded. "Yeah. it's all good. I'm about to become Mrs. McCall." She squared her shoulders and faced her guests and the man she'd been waiting to spend the rest of her life with.

"Ready whenever you are."

Mike waited for Kennedy to take the first step. When she did, they sauntered down the aisle and stopped for the photographer who kneeled near the first row of seats. His eyes swept the left side of the room near the photographer. He could have sworn his heart stopped when he locked eyes with Danielle, who was just as beautiful as she was in his memories of her. The corners of her lips turned up in acknowledgment, though he couldn't be sure if that smile was for him or the bride.

He and Kennedy stopped when they reached the first row of seats. A few whistles came from the audience.

"Who gives this woman to be married to this man?"

Mabel stood, and together, she and Mike said, "We do."

Mike lifted Kennedy's hand and kissed the back of it. He didn't utter another word for fear he'd get choked up. He didn't think seeing Kennedy get married would make him emotional. He walked her a few steps closer and placed her hand in her groom's. Mike turned on his heel and took the seat on the other side of Mabel, which was right in front of Danielle. He locked eyes with her before he sat. He sensed the love between the two of them was still there. Her eyes were soft and welcoming, reminding him of every time she'd said, *I love you.*

It took every ounce of strength he had to sit through the ceremony and not get up and move to the row behind him, just to be near Danielle again. It was pure torture for him to be so close to her and not exchange words, not touch, not look into her beautiful eyes.

Why had he allowed so much time to pass without speaking? Especially considering the near-death experience he'd had. Life was precious, so why wasn't he acting like it?

He focused his attention on the bride and groom. How had they already started exchanging vows? They recited the traditional wedding vows and moved away from the minister to perform the unity sand ceremony. Kennedy hadn't been able to hold back her tears as he encouraged her earlier, but Darius was there to take care of her now. He wiped her cheek with the back of his finger. The look she gave him was one of a woman in love.

He couldn't help himself. He turned away from the ceremony to look behind him at Danielle. His eyes met Bernadette's first. She winked and nudged Danielle's shoulder with her own. They were connected enough to where he knew she felt his eyes on her. Was she ignoring him or just enjoying the ceremony? Their eyes met. She smiled at him and gnawed on her lip. What was it she wanted to say? That had always been a telltale sign she had something she needed to get off her chest.

It had to be the ceremony and the love floating around the room because he couldn't help himself. He mouthed, *I love you.* He didn't care how she would respond, but in case she didn't give him the opportunity to talk when the wedding was over, he wanted her to know he still cared deeply for her. *I love you,* she mouthed back. He gripped his chest because he thought his heart would stop. Satisfied, he turned and gave his attention to Kennedy and Darius, who were now exchanging rings.

"With the power vested in me, for the first time in eternity, I now pronounce you Mr. and Mrs. Darius McCall."

Darius pulled Kennedy close and kissed her—a bit too passionately for Mike's taste. The crowd cheered, and the wedding coordinator dismissed the guests to the reception tables at the far side of the tent. The wedding party posed for more pictures before they joined their guests. For the life of him, Mike couldn't wait to get close to Danielle again. Seeing her today solidified that he never wanted to be without her again.

CHAPTER TWENTY

Danielle's resolve melted when Mike mouthed, *I love you.* She didn't read lips well, but those words she understood. She couldn't be sure if it was the atmosphere or her underlying love for him, but she was in the mindset to make up with him, move on, and maybe have her own happily ever after.

She watched him stand and call everyone's attention so he could toast the newlyweds.

He clinked his silverware against a champagne flute. "May I have your attention, please?"

The room quieted, and everyone shifted their attention to Mike.

"Kennedy, you know you're like a sister to me, and to see you grown up, running a company, and getting married is a little much for me, but you're strong, and I know you can handle whatever comes your way. And Darius, consider yourself a blessed man. Since Kennedy chose you, I believe you to be a loyal and loving man. Take care of each other. Keep God first." His eyes darted to Danielle's when he said, "And be quick to listen, slow to speak, and slow to become angry."

Her heart raced. The tiny hairs on her arms stood, and every muscle in her body clenched. Could she just run up there and kiss him now?

He finished with, "I wish you both an abundant life of happiness. Cheers."

Cheers rang out from the room.

Darius' brother and best man, Andrew, stood next and gave his toast. Andrew told the story of how Kennedy and Darius were practically set up by his mom, who then brought Nina in on her scheme. Soft chuckles echoed throughout the room at his version of the story. Danielle smiled. The love between the brothers was obvious. Made her happy for both Nina and Kennedy marrying into a nice family.

Nina, Kennedy's matron of honor, stood next and also gave a short speech. The brevity surprised Danielle because Nina could be long-winded. She should know. She served as her assistant for eight years.

"When Momma Rose told me about her plan, and I met Kennedy, my matchmaking radar went off. I knew these two would make the perfect couple. Now look at us. Celebrating the newlyweds. You two were made for each other. I think I may be more excited than anyone because I get a sister-in-love." Nina released a tiny squeal and shimmied her shoulders. "But seriously, my heart is happy you two found love in each other. May God bless your union." She motioned to sit but popped up and added, "If anyone else needs my services, come see me after the reception." She glanced around the room, but her gaze stopped at Danielle. Nina raised her glass and reclaimed her seat.

Danielle squinted and shook her head at Nina, who winked in return.

The wedding coordinator announced the newlywed's first dance when the soloists returned to the floor to sing a rendition of Ne-Yo's "Never Knew I Needed." The guests watched the couple groove to the song with their coordinated dance routine. When they finished, they waved their guests to the dance floor. Danielle remained seated next to her mother.

Mike approached the duo and extended his hand to Danielle. She was pretty sure her heart stopped.

"May I have this dance?"

Danielle didn't verbally respond, but placed her hands in his. He stood and led her to the dance floor away from the other guests. He positioned his hands at her waist. She wrapped her arms around his neck. The move was second nature. She thought about it and figured the touch was too intimate and moved to place her hands on his shoulders.

"No."

She gazed up at him.

"Please. I like the feel of your arms around my neck. I miss that."

Thank goodness she wasn't a stick of butter because she would have melted on the spot. The intensity of his eyes.

That special something about his firm but gentle voice. Both were enough to take her down. She stiffened, but not because anything was wrong. In fact, everything was right. And she was afraid her nervousness would make her trip.

They swayed off beat. The music was more of an upbeat tempo, but they moved like it was a slow song.

"Dani, I need to apologize to you."

"No, I need to apologize."

He placed one finger on her lips and shook his head.

"Me first." His gaze remained intense, and she had to fight to keep her knees from buckling. She arched her back a little, hoping that would help.

"I've had a long time to think about everything that happened. Many conversations with my mom. Talked to Thad, too."

She smiled, but didn't interrupt.

"Even though I disagree with how you all handled the situation, I can appreciate that you would go as far as pretending to be my fiancée to help me."

She searched his eyes, waiting for him to bring up the money. When he didn't, she asked. "And what about the money?"

He released a deep sigh. "That's the part I don't like. That made me feel like I was only worth it if money was attached to it, especially after not being with each other for so long. But I know you didn't cash the check. Thad told me. And just to be clear, cashing that check wouldn't stop me from loving you, Dani. Even with everything that's happened, I believe I know you well enough to know that money wouldn't have driven the choices you made."

Danielle rested her head against his firm chest. "Thank you. It means a lot to hear you say that. It broke my heart to think you questioned my character."

She pulled away and made eye contact. Ripples of electrical currents coursed through her body when their eyes connected. It was almost as if their souls intertwined, too. "But all I wanted was to be there for you. And I wanted to tell you about Thad. I just didn't think it was my place to do that. Mike, believe that I didn't like withholding anything from you. I love you. I knew that I still did the moment I saw you when I walked into McCall Resorts' office for the grand opening. But you may not remember that."

"I'm sorry, I don't." He kissed her forehead. "But I would like to make more memories with you."

"I'd like that, too."

"I'm happy to hear you say that because I came across this old box at my house a couple of weeks ago." He reached inside of his tux and removed a small velvet box. "Though I haven't gotten all of my memories back, I seem to remember that I bought this for a very special woman more than five years ago." He popped open the box. "And if there's anything I've learned over the past eight months, it's that I don't want to spend another moment without you. I prefer to work through our issues side-by-side."

He kneeled on one knee. Everything else happening around them ceased, along with the beating of her heart. Tears sprung to her eyes. The stones in the ring blurred. *This is really happening.*

"Danielle Alicia Adams, will you marry me?"

She bobbed her head several times until she found her voice. "Yes, Mike, I'll marry you."

With Every Moment

Mike slipped the ring on her finger, rose, and pulled her into his arms. This time, he crushed his lips against hers. Danielle reveled in the taste of him, every inch of her enjoying the moment. He held her waist, not knowing that was the only thing keeping her from collapsing.

He pulled away and murmured against her lips. "I love you."

"I love you back."

"Finally," someone shouted from behind the couple.

They turned to see the newlyweds, along with Jeffrey and Rose, Nina and Andrew, Mabel and Thad, and Bernadette applauding them.

"Well, Nina, I have to hand it to you: You were right," Kennedy said.

Danielle scrunched her eyebrows. "What are you talking about?"

"She said you would be too stubborn to come, but your mom could talk you into it. If we didn't get you two back together at the wedding, we had backup plans."

Nina shifted Andrew Jr. from one hip to the other and added, "But see, it all worked out. And thank goodness it did because y'all were making us do the most."

Andrew threw his palms up. "Hey, I don't get involved in other folks' love lives."

Darius added, "I'm guilty by association," then he kissed Kennedy's temple.

Rose smiled. "I can't take any credit for this one, but welcome to the family. Both of you."

Mabel stepped forward and threw her arms around the two of them. "I'm so relieved you two worked this out. I'd hate for you to spend forty years apart."

Danielle looked to Mike with hiked brows.

"She's talking about her and Thad."

"Ah, I see. Well, in that case. I'd hate to spend any more time without him."

Mike gave her a quick peck on the lips.

Danielle smiled at the group and shrugged. "I guess I should say thanks for meddling in my business."

Nina returned the smile. "That's what family is for. Welcome."

EPILOGUE

A range of emotions coursed through Danielle. Today, they gathered inside the main house at McCall Resorts once more, but this time to celebrate her. Since getting married last month, Kennedy had quickly gotten used to the whole big family thing, so this whole get-together was her idea.

"Celebration" blasted through the home's speaker system. And while that sounded great in theory, she wasn't one hundred percent sure if this would be a joyous occasion. And to make matters worse, Mike and Kennedy talked her into waiting to open her Uniform Bar Exam results so the family could celebrate her. Though she agreed, she'd been eager to share the news with her new colleagues at Hudson & Stewart. She started as an associate two weeks ago, but the thought of not knowing the results weighed on her–like she wasn't quite equal to everyone else since didn't know if she'd passed the Texas Bar or not.

I should've peeked and resealed the envelope.

Her loves filled the room: Mike, her mom, friends, and new family. The gang sat around the coffee table with smiles covering their faces—smiles so big she had to wonder if they'd opened up the letter and resealed it. As nosey and meddlesome as they were, she wouldn't put it past them. Especially since Mike held on to the letter since it had arrived in the mail yesterday.

Nina jumped out of her seat. "Oh, wait, I almost forgot." She scurried from the room and returned with the letter on a pink glittered pillow. She walked slowly toward Danielle and held the pillow in front of her like a game show model.

"You're so extra."

The group agreed and laughed, which encouraged Andrew Jr. to laugh as well.

"See, even Junior agrees with me."

Nina took her time reclaiming her seat. "Sometimes, *extra* is needed."

Danielle ripped the envelope open.

"Wait," Mabel, Rose, and Bernadette said all at once.

"Great minds think alike. Let's pray first," Bernadette said.

"Father God, we come into Your presence to say thank You for Your many blessings, Your goodness, and Your mercy. Forgive us for when we go our own way and against Your will. We come today to ask that You remind Dani and each of us You are in control no matter what, that You have our best interest in mind to bring glory to Your name. And also help us remember that the plans You have for us are greater than we can imagine. No matter the outcome, we will still praise You. In Jesus' name. Amen."

In unison, they all said, "Amen."

"Okay. My heart is about to beat out of my chest. Does anybody else have anything they'd like to say or do before I open this letter?"

"I do," Mike said. "We're proud of you, and we want you to know we're with you, right?"

Everyone agreed, "Right."

"Thanks." Danielle released a pent-up breath. When she said her heart was beating out of her chest, she didn't lie. She thought it would pop out and go out on its own. She removed the letter from the envelope. The silence in the room was almost deafening. Andrew Jr. took his cues from everyone else because he watched her with an intense stare.

Danielle's shoulders slumped as she read the letter. Mike sat next to her and peered over her shoulder.

"What does it say, baby?" her mother called out.

She kept her voice flat to conceal her emotions. "Congratulations, your Uniform Bar Examination result meets the requirement for admission in Texas."

They jumped and screamed.

Tears filled her eyes. *I did it. Thank You, Lord.*

She didn't see Kennedy leave the room, but she saw her return with a sheet cake covered in white buttercream frosting. The message read, *Congratulations! We knew you could do it!*

Mike pulled her into his arms. Even the firmness of his hold couldn't stop her body from shaking with excitement. Though it took many years to find the courage to even go to law school, take the bar exam and pass, and reconnect with the love of her life, she wouldn't change any of her circumstances. Because with every moment it took to get to this place in her life, she became a better person for it.

Dear reader,

I hope you enjoyed Mike and Danielle's journey back to each other.

As a child, my mom would say, *"The Road to hell is paved with good intentions."* You've probably heard that saying, too. Sometimes, our choices seem right to us, but aren't always perceived that way to the other person involved. Proverbs 14:12 NKJV says, There is a way *that seems* right to a man, but its end *is* the way of death.

I'd like to encourage you to seek God in everything. Like Danielle learned, the easiest/quickest solution is not always the best one. We should all ask ourselves how God would want us to respond or move forward in any situation. Ultimately, Danielle and Mike's situation worked out because she and Mike chose to love and forgive. This is my encouragement to you today: Choose love. Choose forgiveness. Choose the path God would have you take.

I'd love to hear what you thought of this story. Please take a moment to leave a review on Amazon/Goodreads/Bookbub.

Natasha

About the Author

Natasha writes Christian fiction and devotionals. When she isn't reading or writing, she spends her time working out, swimming or watching movies with her family. She lives in the Houston metro area with her husband and three children.

Connect with Natasha online:

Bookbub @NatashaDFrazier

Instagram @author_natashafrazier

Twitter @author_natashaf

Facebook @craves.2012

Website: www.natashafrazier.com

Natasha D. Frazier

Other titles by Natasha D. Frazier

CPSIA information can be obtained
at www.ICGtesting.com
Printed in the USA
LVHW040529070622
720606LV00005B/96